Knight's Rebirth

SARAH ASHWOOD

Knight's Rebirth

Copyright © Sarah Ashwood

Editing by J & J Editing and Marketing Services

Cover art by Stephanie Burdine at Agape Author Services

Interior Design by Savannah Jezowski at Dragonpenpress.com

ISBN: 9781790429844

ALL RIGHTS RESERVED. Excepting brief review quotes, this book may not be reproduced in whole or in part without the express written permission of the copyright holder. The unauthorized reproduction or distribution of this copyrighted work is illegal.

This is a work of fiction. Any resemblance to persons living or dead, real events, locations, or organizations is purely coincidental.

DEDICATION

To my husband, Steven Blackwell

"Once in a while, in the middle of an ordinary life...love gives us a fairytale."
Melissa Brown

Maybe he's not a knight who faces down dragons, but he puts in countless hours at a difficult job for our family, which is just as brave. I'm so proud to be his wife, and I think we've got a pretty good real-life fairytale romance going on.

Here's to happily ever after.

PROLOGUE

Once upon a time there was a faraway land, a beautiful kingdom. Its name was England, and it was part of the British Empire, ruled—as it had been for many years—by the famous Queen Elizabeth.

In this kingdom, a young visitor from a distant land across the sea, a land called the United States of America, made an amazing discovery. Her name was Casie, and she was working as a member of an archeological team excavating the ruins of an ancient castle decimated by war, nature, and time, when she discovered a hidden room that led to a secret library. In this library were many exciting, fascinating books and manuscripts that would set the historical, literary, and archeological worlds abuzz for many years. But the most amazing item of all was that which Casie discovered and put back for herself.

It wasn't much to look at, not like some of the other items in the secret library. Still, when she held the red leather volume in her hands, its pages tinged with gold and its cover embossed with the same, the little book appealed to her. No, it more than appealed to her, it *spoke* to her.

"Casie," it called, "Casie Dillard. Keep me. Read me. If you do, I will change your life, just as I once changed his."

His? His who? she wondered. Then thought, *I must be going crazy. I'm thinking a book is talking to me!*

She was about to lay it aside, to be picked over and studied along with all the other items in the room, when it called her name again.

"Casie. Casie Dillard."

Her head snapped up. *Where's that coming from?*

"Casie?"

The young visitor whirled with a gasp, only to see one of her team members standing in the crumbling, arched doorway.

"George!"

"None other," the young man replied, shouldering into the room.

George was from the ancient kingdom of Britain. To the American visitor, everything about him was British, from his accent, his primness, and his habit of drinking hot tea instead of coffee to his droll sense of humor. Not to mention his name: George Stanton. How typically British. How boring.

Needless to say, Casie was not overly impressed with George, although he was nice enough in a bland sort of way.

"George—did you just call me?" she stammered.

Maybe that's it. Maybe that's what I'm hearing.

"I said your name just now."

"No, I mean before that. Did you say my name, my whole name, and then something about a book?"

Puzzlement clouded the brown eyes shielded by wire-framed glasses. "What are you talking about, Casie?" Then those same brown eyes lighted upon what she clasped in her hands. Instantly, their typical sleepiness dissolved into something else entirely. "Blimey! What have you got there?"

For some reason, inexplicable even to her, Casie did not want to share. She didn't want boring ol' George seeing her prize, her secret discovery. In fact, the longer she clasped it in her hands, the less she wanted to let go. It was as if some sort of spell had been cast over her—possibly by the book itself. A spell that made her protective and possessive, attributes she normally didn't display.

But George had seen it and refused to be dissuaded.

"It's just something I found in here," she answered coolly, trying to pretend the book was really of no consequence. But when her British team member started to reach for it, she snatched it away.

"Uh-uh-uh!" she warned. "First, you have to promise not to tell anyone else about it. Not until I've had a chance to look it over."

"Why?"

Although clearly puzzled, the young man appeared more eager than ever.

"Because...because I said so," she explained lamely. "I found it, and I want to be the first one to study it. Promise, George. Promise, or I won't let you see it."

George merely shrugged, too much of a gentleman to do anything except let her have her way.

"As you like, Casie. Now, may I see it?"

He held out his hands. Reluctantly, Casie slid her precious volume into them, watching him closely for any sign...

It only took a moment. She saw the flicker that passed over his generally unruffled features, the way his sandy blonde head snapped up. Casie didn't have to ask. She knew he'd heard the voice too.

By unspoken agreement, the pair agreed to keep the little volume to themselves. Whereas Casie had originally been reluctant to let George in, she now found him indispensable. It turned out he knew a great deal concerning languages and dialects, both ancient and modern. It took some hard work and many hours of research, but eventually he was able to translate the gold letters that marched proudly across the front of their treasure.

Rebirth of a Knight, they said. Or, as Casie liked to think of it, *Knight's Rebirth*.

After the title was deciphered, the rest fell more or less quickly into place. The two of them became obsessed with their find, and spent hours poring over its pages. Pleased with its captive audience, the book no longer spoke to them, but neither of the pair could forget its sly promise.

I will change your life, it had sworn, *just as I changed his.*

Initially, neither Casie nor George had the slightest idea what this strange vow meant. But, as chapter after chapter of the book was translated, copied down, and saved in a file on Casie's laptop, the meaning became clear. Casie and George were so impressed by the story they were unfolding, that they soon forgot it was scientifically impossible.

Secretly, both began to wonder if, in the dim ages of earth's past, the world described in *Rebirth of a Knight* had actually existed, and if the people in that world had lived and breathed just as the two of them now lived and breathed. Secretly, they questioned whether or not true magic really was an impossibility. After all, hadn't the book spoken to them, just as it did to the man in its pages? Wasn't its spell cast over them too, making them forget everything and everyone besides it?

And each other.

It was Casie who noticed it first, noticed how all the things she'd once found so uninspiring and unattractive in George no longer seemed to matter. How they actually had a lot in common when they got to know one another, and how, as he chuckled over certain passages of the little scarlet volume, he did have a sense of humor. Those brown eyes were not as sleepy as she'd once thought, not when lit with animation as he worked feverishly to translate the next page. Nor when they gazed at her. When they did that, they were soft with admiration and...something else.

It was George who, upon their reaching the description of the first kiss between the man and woman, said to her, "Do you think one kiss can really change so much? Do you think it can bind people together like that?"

And it was Casie who replied very softly, "I don't know, but I'm willing to find out."

Who made the first move they never could decide. All the American visitor knew was that one moment she was sitting beside her colleague, poring over an ancient manuscript, and the next she was in the arms of her fairytale prince. True love's first kiss was, indeed, all it was cracked up to be, she decided, as her heart melted into a puddle of love for George Stanton.

In the end, the book's prediction came true. George left that faraway kingdom of Britain, traveling to another realm across the sea with the young woman who was now his wife. During the ensuing winter months, while Casie's stomach rounded gently with their first child, the two finished transcribing *Rebirth of a Knight*, and readied it for publication.

In due time, it was released to the world. Some accepted it with open arms, others with doubts, criticism, and speculation. For years to come, the world's leading scientists, philosophers, doctors, and professors would debate the authenticity of the tale, some rejecting it out of hand but others pointing out the strange, hitherto unknown language in which it had been written. Debates would rage, but they could not touch the young couple whose lives had been so profoundly altered.

The author's wish at the conclusion of his tale had come true for them. In the grand style of the best and most of famous fairytales, George and Casie were to live happily ever after. As would the twins Casie delivered the following spring, twins whose names had been selected long ago.

Buck and Mercy.

CHAPTER ONE
Of Dragons and Princesses

My name is Buckhunter Dornley, and I am dead.

Dead? You may laugh if you wish. You may write off this statement as a jest or a joke. Or you may simply choose to ignore or disbelieve it. I'm sure most people would. Still, perhaps you should wait before making this decision.

The more I see of life, the more firmly convinced I am that the majority of the populace are content to live their lives in a box of unoriginality. The unknown frightens rather than appeals to them, so they say that this cannot happen and that cannot possibly exist. Once, I too was such a person. There were things that frightened me, so I fled them as swiftly as I could.

Do not allow yourself to be like that. Do not ever be afraid to investigate the unexplored, to set sail on a wild sea, to climb a soaring mountain, or prove by faith that the impossible is possible.

In the end, you must do as you see fit with my strange, unexpected words. It hardly matters to me, for I am, as I have told you, dead. And the dead do not care what others think.

The summer sun's hot rays beat relentlessly upon my chainmail and armor. Inside their metal depths, I would have been baking like a loaf of brown bread, had I not been dead. Despite my deceased state, I felt salty sweat trickle down my protruding spine, my papery skin, and shifted uneasily in the saddle. Beneath me, Stalker, my enormous red-roan steed, caught the vexed bent of my spirits and shifted too. I calmed him with a pat to his wide, strong shoulder, while casting a glance towards the royal box towering over the tournament grounds.

There she sat, so beautiful I felt it like a jolt to my cold, dead bones. Mercy was her name. Her Royal Highness, Mercy Elizabeth Candice Graceknot, princess of the realm. To me, however, she was far more than a long name and a mere princess garbed in silver and blue, the azure veil attached to her golden crown fluttering coquettishly in the breeze. Far more than heavy blonde hair, ocean blue eyes, a pert, upturned nose, and the sweetest smile you've ever seen.

For her, I sat on Stalker's back, awaiting my turn to enter the lists. For her, I wore this heavy armor that bore down my slumped shoulders and made my brittle legs quiver with exhaustion. For her, I kept the visor of my helmet closed. Once she'd loved my face, or so she claimed, but I didn't think she would favor it now. And this too was because of her.

Mercy Graceknot, princess of Merris, the woman

Knight's Rebirth

I'd once loved and sought to marry, was also the person who had slipped a dagger between my ribs and put me in this, well, *dead* state. There was no mistaking my assailant. I knew it was her, for she'd been in my arms at the time. In the midst of a passionate embrace, I had felt a sharp pain in my side and looked down to see a scarlet stream mushrooming from around the blade of a deadly *needle dagger*—so named because of the skinniness of the blade and its resemblance to the seamstress's tool. Clutching the dagger's hilt was a delicate hand I knew very well: Mercy's.

"Mercy, what have you done?" I had cried, swaying on my feet, feeling the strength draining from my limbs along with the blood from my veins.

"Forgive me, Buck," she'd answered, her face white and her lips trembling. Horror was in her eyes, horror both at what she had done and why she'd been forced to do it. "There was no other recourse. I was left with no choice. Please forgive me."

With that, she withdrew the blade only to plunge it again and again into my side. Howling, I had tried desperately to twist away from her savage assault. My warrior's instincts bade me fight back, draw my sword from its sheath and lop off my assailant's head. But I couldn't do that, I couldn't. I could not kill Mercy. I could not harm the woman I loved, no matter that she was clearly resolved to kill me.

She ran me through seven or eight times before I collapsed. Where a blossom like her ever found the fortitude for it, I can't say. Love, I suppose, which fortifies the frail. Not that anyone could accuse my Mercy of fragility—but one hardly suspects a sweet, generous princess of having the resilience to commit murder, either.

Finally, my knees buckling and my arms like lead, I had toppled. My vision swam as my head drooped in defeat.

"Why?" I'd gasped. "Why? I would have found a way..."

I made a final effort to stay upright, my hands groping feebly at the hem of her white gown, now drenched with my blood. "Why, Mercy, why..."

"Forgive me, Buck," she had wept, pulling away from me. All means of support gone, I fell, face in the dirt, tasting gritty soil and coppery blood on my tongue. The last thing I remember as I passed from this life was her plea for exculpation ringing in my ears. "Forgive me, Buck. Forgive me..."

Coming back to the present, I marveled that I could recall all of this so clearly as I stared at her, sitting calm, collected, and composed at her father's side.

How, I wondered, *can she put on such a brave face when she knows the fate that awaits her? How can she look so peaceful with death waiting in the wings?*

But that was Mercy's way. She did not fret and worry as others might. She laughed at trials and scoffed at defeat. During times of blackness and sorrow, she waited patiently for sunshine to part the clouds. Her life's mission was to make others happy, and she bore this heavy burden effortlessly. Taking the hardships of others onto her own slender shoulders, she carried them with the sufferer. She gave of herself, expending all of her energy in the pursuit of happiness—the truest sort of happiness which comes from making other people happy.

For this I adored her while I lived, and for this I

adore her still. It is said the dead cannot feel, but I know that is a lie, for when I gazed at Mercy I felt a love so tremendous that my cold, motionless heart almost began to beat.

From the cliff-ringed pit three hundred paces away a growl interrupted my reverie. Low and sonorous, it rumbled across the jousting field, shaking the earth beneath our feet. Of every warhorse present, Stalker alone was unbothered by the challenge. He'd faced dragons on numerous occasions, and recognized the growl as belonging to an old opponent of ours, Triplehorn Wingback, an enormous male dragon with scales of green and a striped underbelly of red. Silver wings protruded from his back, and three silver horns adorned his head—hence the moniker. We've clashed with him twice, Stalker and I, and both times the match came to a draw.

Today, though, I promised myself, *dead as I am, I shall make a fight with Triplehorn Wingback such as has never been seen, and I will win.*

I had to win. For, you see, if I failed...my Mercy must die.

Dragons and the living dead aside, there was nothing in the world so terrifying as that.

CHAPTER TWO
Of Curators and Wolves

I suppose I ought to return to the beginning of this tale. After all, you, my readers, are probably still confused by its opening. How, you may ask, can a dead man tell a story? A dead man cannot speak or write. How, then, can he return from the grave to relate the circumstances of his past life, and why should he care to? Do the dead care for anything? After all, they are *dead*.

Those are good points, and all true. I am dead, but it is not true that I care for nothing. About some things I still care very much. I care for Mercy. I care for the fight I face with Triplehorn Wingback, and I care that all should know the truth of this account. Many lies have been spread concerning the matter, and before the end comes, I would give a full, verified reckoning.

So, if you care to continue reading, I shall tell you my story from the beginning. It is the story of a man, a knight, a warrior, and the woman he loves. It is the story of a renewal, a restoration, a rebirth.

These things being said, let us now begin...

It was midsummer of the year 1333 in the fourth of age of Gindlon the Bold. Gindlon, as you may remember from your history lessons, was the great explorer who sailed the Nine Seas and discovered my home continent of Gindsland, naming it and claiming it for himself.

On this particular day, I, Sir Buckhunter Dornley, had just won my sixth tournament of the year. Although it was the last of the season, it was certainly not the least. Actually, it was my greatest triumph, for the Tournament of Standing Oak was the most prestigious in all Gindsland, despite being held in tiny Gordinia, sister-kingdom to Merris. These two kingdoms were Gindsland's smallest realms, and when added together the sum total of their lands didn't equal the length and breadth of Fredosia, where High King Delmont dwelt. Speaking of Delmont, who was a direct descendant of Gindlon himself, the High King was present at Standing Oak that day to witness my brilliant achievements in the lists, along with many of the lesser kings who ruled the continent's thirteen kingdoms.

As had come to be expected, I was the undisputed victor of every competition I entered. This was not because of chance or luck. At a young age, I'd been made squire to the High King's champion, a knight by the name of Sir Tirreld. Although my father had cared little for me as his second son, he'd seen my potential as a soldier.

Perhaps he was also thinking of the future money I could earn for him, or of making me his own champion in due time. I had traded swinging rattles as a baby for swinging practice weapons when I was barely past toddlerhood. I'd followed Father's men-at-arms from the time I could walk, fascinated by everything to do with being a soldier, a knight. By the time I was thirteen, I had surpassed what Father's champion could teach me. Sir Dennix had then recommended to Father, "You'd best apprentice the lad to the finest. Because he will be the finest."

So Father had, and so I had become.

By the end of Standing Oak, my purse was stuffed with prize money. My saddlebags were likewise stuffed—not with money, but with silk scarves and satin hair ribbons. Ranging from every color under the sun, they were favors tendered to me by a multitude of very beautiful and very available young ladies. Tied to my lance, to my sword's hilt, to my arm, or to Stalker's bridle, throughout the past few years I'd earned quite the collection. Far more than the average knight garners during a lifetime of fighting. Unlike many of my fellow brothers-in-arms, however, I would far rather have the winner's gold and silver than favors from the ladies.

I suppose I was not as other men. My greatest fear was also my greatest secret: that one of the soft-eyed, curvy creatures should somehow trap me into the honored estate of matrimony. I could not see myself settling down with one woman, giving up tournaments and traveling to raise a brood of dirty, noisy, pesky children. My adventurous life was far too exciting to exchange for the humdrum existence of father and husband.

So, in short, I accepted their favors and nothing more. As quickly as each tournament ended I fled, not giving any black-haired, red-haired, blonde, or brunette maiden the chance to bat her lashes and coax me prettily to join her at a feast in her father's castle. A feast ostensibly to honor my achievements, but in reality for the maiden to work her charms until I was drunk enough to blunder into her trap.

A pox upon such a fate! Before I knew it, I would be cornered and married. (Or are the two one and the same?) A babe would be on the way, and my wife would be pestering me with such tearful statements as, "No, Buck, you mustn't go now. How can you think of tournaments when the baby is coming? Would you really leave me and your forthcoming child? No, I forbid it!"

Definitely not the sort of life for me. I was far too young to be tied down.

In keeping with my past habits, as soon as the last match of Standing Oak had been fought and won, I was on my way. Many a lady was left with red eyes and wet cheeks, but I refused to care. Nothing compared to my freedom, which I was not prepared to surrender.

Four days later, I found myself encamped on the grassy banks of a wide, shallow stream. Lofty trees surrounded the clearing, and vines loaded with berries peeped out from the underbrush. Birds sang, flowers bobbing their heads in time to the music. It was an excellent place to rest, recoup, and reassess my outlook on life. A perfect spot for doing a bit of hunting and fishing, relaxing and daydreaming. I planned to make good use of it.

"Stalker, old friend," I said as I lifted the saddle

from his back and placed it beneath the shade of a towering elm. "What say you to a week or two's rest in the peace of this wide forest? Standing Oak was the last tournament of the season worthy of our talents. We have nowhere in particular to be. We've slain our quota of dragons for the season (I always tried to kill at least three dragons per season), and our old nemesis Triplehorn Wingback has fled to parts unseen. I see no need to bother tracking him down. We've fought him twice, and I find I grow bored with facing the same dragon. Besides, I think we're safe here. Surely no blue-eyed maidens or crafty fathers can find us in these deep woods."

I scratched the noble beast behind the ears. "What say you, my friend? Would you enjoy a time of convalescence?"

Nodding his head fervently as horses will, he seemed to signal agreement. I laughed and set myself to the task of establishing a comfortable camp. "Then that is what we'll do."

For two days, my plans seemed well laid. No greedy, potential fathers-in-law leapt out from behind bushes, and no potential brides marched past in an endless array of swishing skirts. No scheming matrons looked me over with gleaming eyes, assessing my merits as a prospective match for their precious daughters. Stalker and I greatly enjoyed our well-deserved respite.

As I had judged already by the signs, the forest and meadows abounded with game. Meat was plentiful. I trapped hares, snared fowl, and hunted deer for myself, while my horse grazed upon rich grasses blooming with wildflowers. We were well fed. Nothing, it seemed, was going to disturb me in this peaceful place.

Or, so I thought.

As it turned out, in making plans for a restful holiday, I had forgotten to reckon with a famous maxim I was fond of quoting: *Adventure follows the adventurer, desperate need the hero, and war the warrior.*

I suppose neither adventure, desperate need, or war could get along very well without me. On the third day of my sojourn in Merris, I left Stalker back at the campsite and, sword at my hip, set out into the trees to see what was to be seen. Although on a quest of sorts, I was not expecting to meet anything special. So far, these woods lacked the typical poisonous mushrooms, thorny thickets, murky shadows, unnatural creatures, twisted mists, and black trees dripping with moss that one encounters in standard enchanted forests. Which was fine by me. For all my gruff exterior, I was a secret fancier of nature, and to discover only her beauty here would be enough for me.

Alas, in traditional storybook fashion, what I'd not counted on soon caught me unawares.

It was mid-afternoon, the sun was a bit too warm, and the brook ahead looked inviting. Pushing through the bushes lining the bank, I knelt on one knee at the water's edge and made a cup of one hand. Then, filling my palm with water, I brought it to my lips for a drink.

I was drying my hand on my trousers, when a cold voice from behind me said, "And just what do you think you are doing?"

I started violently. I was rarely surprised. How had this person managed to steal up on me? Instinct took over and I whirled, still on the ground, my hand already clasping the hilt of my sword.

"Who are you?" I challenged.

The speaker was a slender man of average height. His robes were the emerald green of new leaves, his eyes an earth brown, and his hair white as snow. For all his benign appearance, danger radiated from the heated glow in those dark eyes.

"I am the Curator, and this is my forest. Why do you trespass on my land?"

"I beg your pardon," I replied, rising to my feet, hand still gripping my sword, "but I was under the impression that this land and its forests belong to King Merl of Merris."

"Hah! That coward? No, you are very much mistaken, Sir Knight. When you passed yon boundary stone you exchanged his domain for mine. This part of the forest belongs to me, and I want you off my land." His eyes narrowed to pinpricks. "Now."

As taken aback as I was to hear the old vulture call the king a coward, I didn't question him about it. I was too annoyed by his domineering attitude. Who did he think he was to order me about? Me, the famous Sir Buckhunter Dornley?

"You'd best guard your tongue, Curator," I admonished sternly. "If you wish me to leave, demanding I do so is not the way to go about it. Or have you any idea with whom you speak?"

"I would not care if you were the High King himself. I want you gone, and I do not mean tomorrow."

Stubborn since the day of my birth, I stepped closer, looking down my nose into his upturned face, unabashedly using my greater size and height as an added menace. "Were I you, I do not think I would speak so to the most celebrated knight in all of Gindsland."

The hint struck home. The Curator flinched visibly, but retreated behind a wall of anger to hide his dismay.

"So you are Sir Buckhunter Dornley. Well, what is that to me? I still want you to leave."

"Perhaps if you were to ask politely..."

"Perhaps if you were not such a swaggering, imperious braggart..."

This was getting us no place. In heated silence, we glared at one another until I finally said, "Give me one good reason why I should leave, Curator, and I will."

At first, he simply stared at me. Then, a slow, calculating smile crept across his face. "Because," said he, "of what is behind you."

What the deuce?

I whirled, already drawing my sword. Lucky for me that I was, too. The wolf crouching a mere five paces away was huge, half again as big as any I'd seen. It was also green, as green as the forest from whence it had come, as green as the Curator's robes. Both eyes glowed an evil, unnatural red, and it was undoubtedly a master of stealth, just like its master. How they'd managed to sneak up on me was a blow to my pride, but I had no time to contemplate the insult, for with a word from its owner—"Attack!"—the beast did just that.

Leaving its crouch smoothly, the monster sprang at me. I dodged, feinting to the left, grateful for well-honed reflexes. I'd barely time to set my feet before—with some impressive reflexes of its own—the green wolf landed, spun, and leapt at me again. This time I whirled as I dodged, turning my wrist in a circle as I swung at the wolf. I managed a slice along the beast's ribs, one that elicited a howl of pain but probably caused more anger than damage.

We squared off, facing one another warily. I now boasted his blood on my sword, while he'd yet to touch me. This gave him pause, and I wasn't about to attack him first.

The Curator spoke up. "Your skills are worthy of their praise, Sir Knight. No one else could have lasted so long against my pet. Nevertheless, I would warn you that he's never been bested."

I flicked a glance his way. He was standing there grinning madly. He found this amusing? I could have killed him for that, and vowed to, just as soon as I finished off his weird wolf.

"Give it up, Curator," I snapped. "Call off your wolf. Do it now, while it merely bleeds a little."

"No, I do not think I will. You asked for this, by refusing to leave when ordered. I gave you fair opportunity, but you would not take it. Now you must pay the penalty for trespassing on my land and stealing water from my brook."

"Trespassing? Stealing?" I wanted to echo indignantly, but just then the wolf took another flying leap.

This time, rather than dodge, I tried another tactic. When he launched himself into the air, I launched my own body forward and dove *under* him. If an animal's face can register surprise, this wolf's did as his prey suddenly disappeared beneath him. His expression might have been comical had I not been intent on survival. I rolled as I hit the ground, bounding to my feet at the same moment the wolf's forepaws struck earth. He spun, but I was too quick. My sword was already raised and descending.

Fear flooded those wicked, canine eyes. He whimpered like a puppy. My sword thrust was true. The battle was over.

The beast surrendered without a sound, crumpling to the forest floor. Bracing myself with a boot to his massive shoulder, I freed my sword, wiping its blade clean on the beast's odd, emerald fur. Only afterward did I turn to the Curator, who stood there gawking in shock.

"And that," I said, "is the penalty you must pay for attempting to murder me by way of your wolf."

His jaw agape, he uttered a pitiful moan, blinking back tears.

"I was going to leave," I reminded him coldly. "I truly was. I simply wanted you to ask politely."

I'd nothing more to say to the old man. Although an angry part of me insisted I ought to teach the fellow a lesson, I figured the death of his pet was lesson enough. He appeared so badly shaken that I dared to believe any future visitors would be received with much greater kindness.

Sheathing my weapon, I gave him a final, cutting glare before turning on my heel and walking away. I heard the whispers of his robes, the creak of his knees, as he rushed to the dead wolf and dropped beside it. I did not look back, not even when I heard him shout after me, "This is far from over, Buckhunter Dornley. Because my forest did not kill you, do not think you will find safety in Merl's. There is more to his kingdom than meets the eye."

I ignored him, taking his words for the ravings of a lunatic.

"This is not over, Dornley," he shouted. "Not over, not over, not over..."

Eventually, the echoes of his threats and sobs faded into the distance. I was more than happy to leave them behind.

CHAPTER THREE
Of Death or Sleep

That incident spoiled the remainder of my afternoon and evening, but by the following day I had decided to forget it. After all, if what the Curator claimed was true, my campsite must be inside King Merl's domain, which should protect me from tiresome old wizards and their strangely colored pets. So far, nothing I'd encountered in this part of the forest held any kind of threat. I had come here to relax, and that is what I intended to do.

Little did I know, however, that what I met next would prove a far greater threat to my way of life than any elderly Curator or wicked green wolf.

One lazy afternoon, having nothing better to do, I allowed myself to drift off to sleep just out of sight of my tent. My head was pillowed on a saddle blanket and my horse grazed nearby. The sun was warm, as was the grass beneath me. Fully relaxed, I slept. Or intended to sleep. Unfortunately, a very unforeseen, very untoward interruption occurred soon after I'd closed my eyes, awakening me from a light slumber and pleasant dreams.

First, I heard footsteps. Then, "Good gracious!" a voice exclaimed. A female voice. "Will you look at that? I do believe the poor man is dead!"

"Oh, for pity's sake, Rosy," answered a second feminine voice, "he most certainly is not."

"And how would you know?" countered the first. "You've never seen a dead man."

"No, but I have seen many a sleeping one, and I say this one sleeps."

"That makes no sense, Stazia. Why would a man choose to sleep beside a stream, out in the wild where insects could crawl on him, when he could be resting in a comfortable inn instead?"

A sigh from Stazia. "I'm sure I don't know. Here, let us ask the princess—perhaps she will know."

"A fine idea," the one named Rosy concurred. I kept perfectly still, hoping the meddlesome creatures would leave me be, and cringed as I heard her shrill, "Oh, Princess! Princess Mercy! Come and see what we've found."

"If he was asleep, your shouts ought to have awakened him," grumbled the one called Stazia.

She had a point, but I continued to lay still in hopes that they would decide I was dead and be on their way, when I heard,

"What? What have you found?" came a soft, pretty voice, heralding the rustle of feet through fallen leaves.

She approached hastily, but stopped, uttering a cry. "Oh!" A clapping sound, as if she'd clapped her

Knight's Rebirth

hands to her mouth. Then, and very softly, she whispered, "A man...a man in my father's woods." In the ensuing pause, I pictured her glancing from one companion to the other. "Is he dead, do you suppose? Or does he sleep?"

Foolish women! I fumed, keeping as motionless as possible. *How could anyone be so dense they cannot discern a sleeper from a corpse?*

"Stazia says he sleeps, but I say he is most certainly dead," Rosy declared.

"No, he isn't dead," Stazia argued. "He can't be. How can you be so ridiculous, Rosy? Look! I swear his chest rises and falls.

"Princess," she went on, addressing that lady for confirmation, "what say you? Does the handsome man sleep, or is he dead?"

"Hmmm," Princess Mercy mused, and I imagined her cupping her chin in her palm, regarding my tranquil form with an air of thoughtfulness. "You are quite right in one thing, Stazia. He is handsome. However, from this distance, I cannot discern his state of health. Which means—"

She broke off, but the sounds of shoes and swishing skirts told me she was coming closer to investigate.

Go away, woman! I cried mentally, but of course she didn't hear. The next thing I knew, someone was kneeling by my side. Tentatively, a hand touched my cheek, unshaven for the past three days. A woman's soft fingertips grazed the dark whiskers lightly.

"Sir Knight...Sir Knight, are you well?"

Surreptitiously, I clenched my fists at my sides, hoping she wouldn't notice. Hoping she would simply *go away* so I would not have to speak to her, either to reassure her or chase her off.

Her hand moved from my cheek, placing itself boldly on my chest as if to feel for breath. "Sir Knight?" she said, a bit more boldly than before. "Come, man, are you drunk? Injured? Tell me what ails you."

She released a sharp sigh, her annoyance plain. For some perverse reason this pleased me, but the pleasure didn't last long.

"Very well!" she exclaimed. It wasn't difficult to visualize the girl drawing herself up to her full height. "Very well, then. You leave me no recourse." In an authoritative voice, she said, "Whether you are sleeping or dead, I do not know, but I command you to awaken and come back to life. You must do so because I am the princess of this land, and you will obey me."

Then, to my utter astonishment, the hand on my chest lifted, only to—*Would you believe it?*—slap me across the face! The reckless audacity—striking a sleeping knight you do not know!

There was no more feigning sleep in hopes the trio would give up and go away. She'd dug her own grave, and I was prepared to toss her in it. Her companions would be next.

Awakening with a shout, I shoved upright, gaining my feet in a single bound. "Foolish woman!" I roared. "What in Gindlon's name do you think you're doing?"

To my left and right, the two young women who'd originally chanced upon me emitted identical gasps, danced backwards several steps, and clapped identical hands over identical mouths. They were twins, one as alike as the other. Had the first not worn blue and her sister pink, I would've thought my eyes played tricks on me, showing me two of the same woman.

"Have you no common sense," I bellowed, "to meddle with a man you do not know? A stranger, clearly a warrior? Why, I ought to kill the three of you and throw your bodies off yon cliff where they will rot and molder, never to be discovered except by vultures hunting a meal!"

That did it. They were so frightened I could see the whites around two pairs of green eyes. As one, the twins whirled and dashed off into the trees, shrieking in fear, utterly forgetting their companion and any potential danger she might be in.

"Well, that was very rude, I must say," came a voice from my feet. I started, having momentarily forgotten the princess who'd slapped me and ordered me back to life.

"Are you still here?" I growled, my gaze swinging downwards. I'd hoped she would have also taken flight by now.

"What a silly question," she returned, batting long, curled eyelashes. "Of course I am still here, else I would not be speaking to you." She rolled her eyes, adding, "Ninny."

What?

Jamming my fists on my hips, I glowered down at her. "Don't call me that."

She regarded me with coolly. "I am the princess of Merris, and I shall call you whatever I wish."

"Insult me, then," I countered, "and I shall—"

"You shall do nothing, for I am the princess of Merris, while you are nothing but a mere knight, one of many like those my father employs at his castle."

She rose to plant her hands on her hips, glaring fearlessly into my eyes. "Try something, Sir Knight. Rosy and Stazia are even now on their way to the castle, where they will spread word of a strange knight in the woods. Father will send a detachment of his own knights to investigate. If any harm has befallen me, they will take you and throw you into a dungeon to await trial. You'll be pronounced guilty, taken out in the public square, and hanged for all to see. How will your threats and surliness serve you then?"

I'm ashamed to confess that during this lengthy speech my arms had fallen to my sides and my mouth stood agape. *The audacity!* I seethed, unable to say a single word. Had this maiden no shred of common sense? Why hadn't she run, like her lady's maids? How could she stand there and trade words with me—*me*, Sir Buckhunter Dornley, whom kings and dragons alike feared to provoke? Could this possibly be the hidden danger besetting King Merl's kingdom to which the old Curator had referred? She didn't appear threatening, but her brassiness was enough to put any man on his guard.

"Furthermore," she went on, shaking a slender forefinger in my face, "you cannot harm me, for I brought you back to life. You should be grateful, not angry."

"What?" I sputtered, finally regaining my senses. "You did not bring me to life. I wasn't dead."

"Yes, you were," she disagreed, folding her arms across her chest. "I saw you, and you were dead."

"You saw me asleep...or pretending to sleep," I admitted gruffly.

"You *were* asleep, or unconscious. You had to

have been, to sleep through the twins' noise like you did, and you should not be such a grouch," she stated with great finality. Thoroughly unafraid, she stepped back to give me a searching up-and-down inspection.

"My, you are tall, aren't you? I thought so, seeing you laid out as you were. Still, it's always easier to tell a man's height when he's alive and upright than when he is lying down dead."

"For the last time, I was not dead!" I insisted, following her as she swung around and started walking away.

She threw a teasing grin over her shoulder. "Of course you weren't."

Gaining the top of a small hill, she halted, turning about to face me. Hands folded at the waist, she tipped her head far, far back and grinned up at me.

"Well, it was a pleasure meeting you, Sir Knight, and an even greater pleasure to save you from the sleep of death. I myself will sleep quite well tonight, knowing what good I did today."

I clenched my jaw, preparing to offer a cutting remark on the state of her mental health, but she forestalled me with a cheery, "I must away, and quickly, to the castle. Father will have to be reassured that you mean no harm; that Stazia and Rosy were simply being hysterical again."

Glancing furtively from right to left, she shielded her mouth with a hand while leaning close to murmer—which I had to stoop to catch, "Though I love those twins dearly, I must confess they are prone to fits and apt to try anyone's patience."

I blinked in astonishment, thinking something along the lines of, *It takes one to know one.*

She touched the back of my sword-hand in a gesture of farewell. "A good day to you, then. I will return after I speak with Father. Well, perhaps I'd best wait until tomorrow. Nevertheless, I shall return...you may depend upon it!"

With that, she turned about and loped off into the trees, disappearing down a forest trail in a matter of seconds. Dumbfounded, at a complete loss for one of the first times in my life, I stood there with my hand gripping the hilt of my dagger, gaping after what I could only assume must be an utterly mad young woman.

CHAPTER FOUR
Of Breakfast

*I*f you have continued to read this far, I thank you. However, perhaps you are confused.

"Who is this man?" you may be thinking. "This rude, arrogant man who has little to no liking for anyone but himself?"

If that's what you are thinking, you're absolutely right. I was arrogant and rude, and I cared next to nothing for the thoughts or feelings of others. Perhaps this was due to my upbringing, of having a father who cared nearly nothing for me. Self-preservation was a way of life to me, and it had hardened me. I was a fool, though, as the young maiden around whom my tale centers would soon teach me.

Bear with me. Remember the title of this tale, Rebirth of a Knight? Remember that I claimed that this was not merely the story of a knight's rebirth, but of a man's renewal? Well, that's exactly what it is. Have patience, and in due time you will understand everything.

That night, the night after my first encounter with the bewildering, frustrating princess of Merris, I crawled into my tent for some sleep. Before diving under the covers I shucked off my boots and tunic, then went about the business of making myself comfortable in my bedroll. After nestling about a moment or two, seeking the most restful spot, I finally released the iron grip over my senses and gave myself over to rest.

Banging and clanging awakened me the next morning, startling away the final fragments of a horrendous vision. The dream fled even as I opened my eyes, bolting upright in the blankets. My chest was rising and falling in time with my pounding heart. I couldn't remember what, exactly, I had dreamed, but there had been a woman saying she deserved fine, expensive gifts even while the manor roof was crumbling over our heads and a babe in my arms screamed hysterically.

Gindlon preserve me, I thought, scrubbing a hand over my face to wipe away sleep.

My next thought was, *What is that noise?*

The banging and clanging outside my tent was the noise of pots and utensils rattling, and I could smell the delicious aromas of breakfast cooking.

Surely, I'm still dreaming, I told myself, rubbing my eyes briskly. If I was, this was certainly a far different, and far better, dream than that from which I'd awakened.

Or was it?

To my dread, the next thing I heard was, "Yes, you are a good boy, aren't you?" A woman's voice. I could hear the smile in it. "Good boy, sweet boy, good horse..."

The princess!

Furious, I shoved the blankets away, my vision obscured in a veil of rage. Gritting my teeth, I pulled on my boots and tugged a fresh tunic over my head as fast as I could. Dressed, I pushed the flaps of my tent aside and saw her standing there, a wooden spoon clasped in one hand while the other busily scratched Stalker behind the ears.

"What a sweet boy," she crooned, now stroking his jaw and caressing his neck. "Yes, nothing like your ill-tempered master, are you? No, not at all."

And Stalker—the traitor—pushed his nose into her palm and rubbed his muzzle against her shoulder, enjoying every bit of her attention.

Blasted horse.

I could stand it no longer. "What do you think you're doing?" I barked, bursting out of my tent in a manner I hoped she'd find intimidating, if not downright frightening.

"And a very good morning to you, Sir Knight," she responded brightly, turning and flashing me a sweet smile. I'd failed to fluster her in the least. "I've kept my word and returned as promised. Your fine, friendly horse was keeping me company while I waited on you to arise."

"He is neither fine nor friendly," I retorted, pacing over. How it galled me that this...this woman had not only risen before me, but was waiting on me to awaken! Grabbing Stalker by the halter, I jerked him rudely away. "He is a warhorse, meant for one purpose only: to assist in battle. Stalker can kill, too. Has killed many a time."

"What, this magnificent creature kill? I cannot believe it."

She was goading me, and, unfortunately, I was easily goaded.

"Try," I muttered, leading Stalker out of my campsite and over to a stout tree where I picketed and left him.

Returning to where Mercy of Merris stood, I planted my fists on my hips and glowered down at her: a disturbing new habit I seemed to have acquired lately.

"What are you doing here? Does your father know you traipse about the forest, disturbing sleeping knights?" I bent closer, putting my nose in her face. "Should you not be chaperoned, my lady?"

"Why, Sir Knight," she blinked innocently. "*Need* we be chaperoned?"

Biting off a curse, I wheeled away before I lost my temper. Stomping over to a nearby boulder, I plopped down heavily. There I sat in silence, my arms folded across my chest, brooding.

Ignoring my ire, Princess Mercy went about her task, all the while humming a blithe, happy tune that set my nerves on edge. When I peeked up to see what she was doing, I saw she was indeed cooking. Cooking, uninvited, with my utensils, my pots, and my food too, undoubtedly. Not only this, but she was wearing my red tunic over her plain, brown frock, using it as an apron! Imagine, my war-stained tunic being commandeered by some chit as a kitchen accessory! I bristled with anger, grinding my teeth to keep from swearing, and turned my back on this infuriating creature lest I be forced to do her bodily harm.

How dare she? I fumed, clenching and unclenching my fists in rage. *Anyone, especially a princess, should have a greater sense of propriety.*

After a time, I heard footsteps. She walked over, poking me in the shoulder.

"Sir Knight?"

"What?" I snapped, deliberately keeping my back to her.

"I have prepared breakfast. Do you wish to eat?"

"No!" I said firmly.

Unluckily, my stomach chose that exact moment to growl loudly.

She snickered. "Of course you don't." And before I knew what was happening, she'd slipped around in front of me to push a full plate in my face. "Here you are...breakfast."

I studied her offering suspiciously before raising my hands to take it. "What is this?" I questioned, balancing the meal on one knee while accepting the fork she offered.

"Try it. It's delicious."

"Hmmm." I regarded her warily. "Your assurances mean nothing. Why should I trust you?"

She tilted her head, a faint smile playing about her lips.

"Because I am a trustworthy person? I promised yesterday to return, even though you did nothing to make me welcome, and I kept my word. That means I am trustworthy, which also means you can safely try the breakfast I have cooked."

Her gentle teasing took me aback, perhaps

because of the ring of truth to her words. For whatever reason, she had returned, even though our first encounter had been far from welcoming, to say the least. Either she was brave as a knight or madcap as a hare. Whatever she was, I found myself staring as if truly seeing her for the first time.

I judged her to be about eighteen or nineteen years of age. She was quite short. When we faced one another, the top of her head did not even meet the level of my shoulder; but then, I was quite tall. She was rounded in all the right places, her servant's frock shielding eye-catching curves. Her hands may have been small, but her fingers were long and slender. Golden hair, its radiance slightly dimmed by hints of brown, was braided and coiled around the top of her head like a crown. Her eyes were merry and blue, her mouth generous and pink, and her pert nose made the more interesting by a slight bump in the bridge.

She was pretty, I admitted grudgingly, if one liked short, curvy, brownish-blonde princesses with sapphire eyes and teeny bumps in their noses. Certainly, there was nothing about her appearance to suggest she was untrustworthy. Still, the crux of the matter wasn't that I didn't *trust* her—I just didn't *like* her. My personal opinion of the princess notwithstanding, the food she offered smelled far too appetizing, and my stomach was far too empty, to deny myself.

Not bothering to address her remarks, I scooped up a man-sized bite from the pile on my plate, and shoveled it into my mouth. I was half hoping the food would be disgusting, which would afford me an excuse not to eat it and even to send her away.

No such luck. As she'd promised, it was

delicious.

Smiling, the princess watched the meal vanish. "More?" she inquired when I'd consumed the final bite.

I swiped the back of my fist across my mouth and rubbed the grease onto the fabric of my trousers.

"I suppose," I consented grudgingly, twisting from the waist to watch her walk back to her—my—fire, and dish up a second round of cuisine. What she was serving me, I didn't know. Something with eggs and bread and bacon and strange flecks of green leaves, but it was extremely tasty. My skills at cooking were far overshadowed by my skills in the lists. I'd eaten nothing so delicious in weeks, and devoured the next plateful as readily as the first.

Sated at last, I licked my fingers after setting both plate and fork in the grass beside the boulder. Princess Mercy, having seated herself on the ground before me, wrapped both arms around her knees. She rested her chin against her kneecaps, regarding me with a knowing twinkle in those wide blue eyes. Her gaze made me uncomfortable. I felt as if she saw right through my gruff sham, sensing my every weakness and fault.

"Will you not have some?" I finally asked, nodding towards my plate, casting about for something to break the silence.

She shook her head. "I think not. I ate an apple this morning, and sampled some of your breakfast while I was cooking it." She paused. "I need to lose weight, so I try to curb my appetite for fattening foods. They'll be the death of me yet."

I couldn't help it. I barked a laugh. "You? Lose weight? That is ridiculous."

She pushed herself up, her cheeks flushed with anger. "And what would you know? You could stand to lose some weight yourself!"

"What?" I glanced down at my body. There was no excess weight upon my person. These past few days of relaxation aside, I spent nearly all my time fighting or training to fight, took care with what I ate, drank very little ale or mead, and kept myself in prime physical condition. I was tall, my body heavy with muscle, but muscle was all it was heavy with, and of this I superciliously informed the princess of Merris.

She merely cocked an eyebrow with that infuriating skill all women possess, in which their manner plainly says, *Well, think what you want, but I know better.* As if they are privy to certain insights of which you, as a man, remain ignorant.

I hate it when women do that. And, to a person, they all seem to. No wonder I had never married.

"It's true!" I proclaimed hotly, wishing she would stop looking at me that way. Somehow, it made me feel about two inches tall and two years old.

The eyebrow lowered, but her next cool remark hardly raised my self-esteem. "As you wish," she replied breezily.

That was all she said, but it was easy to interpret what she meant.

I still know better but, in order to avert a fight, I'll let you have your way.

Another peeve of mine. Where do women learn such condescension? At their mother's knee? Or are they all born with the knack of belittling a man and his manhood in such perfectly painful ways?

"If you were a man, you wouldn't make such

ridiculous remarks," I told her. "If you were a man, you would see I'm a warrior and have the body of one. I most certainly am not fat."

"And were you a woman," she returned, unperturbed, "you might realize many women don't favor men so muscled up that they seem pudgy in appearance."

"I don't seem pudgy."

"Yes, you do."

"No, I do not, nor do I care what women favor."

"Then why are you so offended by my statement?"

"I am offended because it is untrue!"

"Is that so?"

She rose to her feet and I rose to mine. My fists were clenched at my sides. I was prepared to do verbal battle for the sake of my muscles' honor, but she was done debating.

"Well, Sir Knight—by the way, what is your name? I've told you mine, yet you neglected to return the favor."

"Dornley," I mumbled sourly. "Buckhunter Dornley."

"Sir Buckhunter Dornley," she repeated, a hesitant catch to the words, as if she tasted them on her tongue. "Hmmm...an interesting name, that. Rather a mouthful, isn't it?"

"I have never found it so."

"You wouldn't, but then, you need not address yourself often, need you? Unless you talk to yourself, and that is a bad habit you must break, for people will think you mad."

Bewildered, I couldn't think of a rejoinder to her teasing quickly enough, and she rushed on, saying,

"Might I call you Buck? For that's what you call to mind."

"Buck?" I rolled my eyes skyward. "I make you think of a deer?"

"A buck-deer, not a doe," she smirked, clasping her hands behind her back and rocking forward on her toes. "A doe is quiet and elegant," she continued, as if I knew nothing on the subject. *Ha!* Was I not one of the ten greatest hunters in the empire? Had I not many a stag's head mounted on my mansion wall? Well, when I had a mansion wall I would mount my collection thereon. Anyway, did I not—

"While a buck," she prattled on, impervious to my drifting thoughts, "rattles his antlers, paws the earth, and puts on a stupendous show to impress his female counterparts.

"Is that what you are doing, Sir Buck?" she added impishly. "Acting like your namesake? Putting on an exhibition of male strength and grouchiness to impress me because I am the only female present?"

"What?" I exploded, having taken all I could. "I'll have you know, Mercy, princess of Merris, that my saddlebags are stuffed with favors from women, peasants and noblewomen alike, who would thank the heavens above every single day if only I'd consent to court them. I've never put on a show to impress them, and I will certainly never put on a show to impress you. I would rather die lonely and alone, a surly, irritable old gaffer in a gusty cottage than be your beau."

Covering her mouth with her hand, she snickered in a way that made me see red.

"It's true!" I snarled, incensed beyond belief.

"Oh, Sir Buck," she gasped, laughing outright,

"you are too, too funny." She dropped her hand. "Enjoy your saddlebags stuffed with favors, then. Enjoy also your gusty cottage and lonely campsite, for I must be away."

"Good! You will not hear me complain."

"But not for long," she warned, brushing a windblown strand of hair out of her eyes. "I shall return on the morrow. After all, I cannot let your stay in my father's woods be lonely. As his daughter, I've an obligation to see to the care of our guests."

"I am not your father's guest, and I wish you would see to the care of someone else. I need nothing from you."

"Not even my cooking?"

"I—" That was enough to give me pause, for her cooking had been superb.

She smiled sympathetically.

"I see how it is, and I shan't deprive you of something you so greatly enjoy. Until tomorrow, then."

As before, she wheeled about, picked up her skirts and loped away, disappearing into the trees. Not until both she and the sounds of her departure had faded did I realize something important. Something terrible enough to spoil my entire day, as even my battle with the Curator's wolf had not spoiled my day.

She'd taken my red tunic, my favorite red tunic, with her. Now I had no choice but to accept her visit on the morrow, for I must have my tunic back. With a heavy heart, but a full stomach, I turned away to tidy up the breakfast mess she'd left for me. It seemed another encounter with that silly woman was unavoidable.

CHAPTER FIVE
Of Firemagic and Warhorses

What does it take for a man to change his mind, especially when it concerns something about which he feels very strongly? Perhaps an accident? Perhaps the brutal truth striking him in the face like an iron-gloved fist? Perhaps a tragedy? Perhaps an instant of sheer happiness? Perhaps the sorrow, or the joy, of another person's presence?

I cannot answer this question for anyone else. In my case, what caused me to change my mind was something very simple indeed. As you will see, what was the beginning of an entirely new viewpoint was nothing more than a change of mood for a certain vivacious princess with a mouth as large as a dragon's den and a heart as big as the open sky.

I'd never known a woman to rise so early; in fact, I was under the impression that most of the fairer sex, due to their delicate disposition, spent nearly every morning sleeping in. When I awakened at dawn, however, there she was, the cheerful princess, sitting on a log I'd placed beside my rock-ringed campfire for that very purpose. Mornings in Merris were subject to be chilly year round, and today a cloak of blue wool was wrapped around her shoulders, its edges clenched in her small fist. A pensive expression furrowed her ivory brow, drawing her slender eyebrows into a "v" of anxiety.

I had quietly poked my head from the tent flaps to observe the princess at her stationary post. Truly, it was the first and only time I'd seen her so subdued. Even Stalker, stealing up to gently nudge her shoulder with his nose, failed to garner a reaction. Instead, with a melancholy sigh, she leaned her cheek against the horse's head. Much to my astonishment, Stalker stood still, content to let her rest against him.

Something must be wrong, I decided, a little surprised by the twinge of fear that creased my guts. Something wrong with chatty, happy-go-lucky, feathers-impossible-to-ruffle Mercy of Merris? *Whatever could have caused that must be foul indeed*, I thought as I climbed from the tent.

Hearing the noise of my exit, she raised her head and gave me a smile. But it was a wan, forlorn sort of smile, quite unlike the teasing grins I was accustomed to receiving from her. This only furthered my suspicions. A warrior can sense when something is amiss. Often, he must rely on these skills when something that on the surface appears normal is altogether wrong. Dealing with Princess Mercy may not have been as life-threatening as leading troops into battle, but simply being in her presence made me wary. Now that something seemed off, I was on my guard again, but it was a different sort of defensiveness. What evil could possibly affect this woman in such a way, and would it affect me, as well?

What ails you, Princess? I wanted to ask. Instead, I offered her a simple, "Good morning."

She nodded a pleasant greeting. "I trust you slept well?"

"I did, thank you," I returned with utmost politeness. The most polite I'd been to her, I realized with a stab of guilt. She could be vexing, but she was also a highborn lady. Perhaps I should have controlled my temper, should have acted in a more gentleman-like manner towards her. She was, after all, a princess.

Feeling somewhat repentant, I knelt before the pile of cold ash and cinders: all that remained of my blazing campfire the night before. She'd not bothered stirring it to life, as she had yesterday. Nor had she bothered to cook me breakfast. I must admit, I was a little disappointed by that.

"Chilly this morning, is it not?" I asked, rubbing my forearms to lower the goosebumps. My cloak lay forgotten in the tent. I would either need to build a fire or go fetch it.

"A little," she answered in a monotone.

I frowned. She was so unlike herself that it made me uneasy. I decided if I could not help her, I could at least build a fire to warm us both, which would also give me something to do besides drive myself to fretting over her. Especially when I didn't know why I was fretting over her. However, when I checked my supplies, I realized I was out of kindling and swore, forgetting the presence of a lady.

This made the princess's head snap up. "Whatever is the matter?"

"I'm out of kindling," I grumbled, "and I was going to build you a fire. I meant to fetch some last night before I fell asleep and it slipped my mind."

She rolled her eyes. "That's too little of a thing to merit cursing," she rebuked mildly, catching me by the arm and preventing me from rising.

"Not if you wish a fire to warm yourself by," I contradicted, puzzled that I'd gotten off with such a mild scolding for the profanity.

"A fire is easy to produce, even without kindling," she said. "Here, I'll show you."

Sliding off the log, she knelt with me beside the ring of charred rocks. Rolling her right shoulder to free it of the cloak, she extended her bare arm and splayed her fingers wide over the cinders. When she did, the skin of her arm brushed mine, and I started at the unexpected contact. My head whipped her way; I found myself mesmerized by her lively profile. She hadn't seemed to notice. Her eyes were transfixed on fingers, hand, and ashes. *I* noticed, though—could think of nothing else—and a part of me I'd never met before sprung to life. A part that was suddenly enthralled by a woman's nearness and the feel of her skin touching mine. I hardly dared breathe, lest the moment slip away and I lose the physical contact.

"*Mrel-tah kornbay* spark and fire," she mumbled, dragging my attention from her soft skin and pretty, feminine scent to what she was doing. "*Mral-kay sorden* and wood."

I was shocked when, a heartbeat later, flame exploded from that pile of ashes and black cinders, kindling itself into burning brightly. The heat washed over us both. My breath hissed in my teeth, and Mercy turned her face up to mine, grinning proudly.

"I told you there was no need for kindling."

"How did you do that?" I demanded, filled with newfound astonishment of a different sort. "How? Are you a magician or a witch?"

"No, not at all," she chuckled, shaking her head while extending her hands to the blaze.

Cautiously, I did the same, both of us warming our hands at her magical inferno.

Heat, smoke, red-orange flames, red coals...feels like a real fire, I assessed, casting dubious glances her way. How had she done that?

"There are many classifications of magicians, Sir Buck, just as there are many ways of working with magic." She flipped her hands over, palms up, warming her reddened knuckles. "When true magicians enter the world, the gift of magic already lies within. Inborn, as it were. They are able to use it as they wish. It is merely another skill, a talent, like the talent some folk have for playing musical instruments."

"And are you not one of these?"

In spite of myself, I was fascinated. Here I'd been thinking her a silly twit, probably capable of nothing more brilliant than, well, annoying and cooking. Now I discovered she was actually capable of creating magical flames, and intelligently discussing the various forces of magic. What other secrets did she hide?

"I'm not. I possess no magic, but I am able to manipulate the forces of magic to a certain extent."

"Manipulate..."

"The forces of magic," she repeated, nodding.

"Yes. You see, Sir Knight, magic is everywhere. It is in the earth, the sky, the soil, the plants, the forest, the mountains. It is in the storm, the whirlwind. In flame and snow and water and rain. It is an invisible force, permeating everything. Where it comes from, who can say? But if you know the right words to speak, you can sometimes entice it into revealing itself."

She motioned towards the fire she'd built using nothing more than a few bizarre words and the machinations of her clever fingers. "What you saw as merely a heap of ash, I saw as an old campfire still retaining a spark of firemagic. Not much, mind you, only a spark, but enough that I was able to coax it into fuller life."

Now it was my brows knit in a frown, my forehead furrowed in thought. "But how does it burn? There's no wood."

"It burns from magic, you silly man," she explained with a laugh, like it should be obvious. "From the magic of the flame.

"However," she advised, "like all fires, this one will not last forever. Pretty soon, you'll have to feed it with wood to keep it going."

I shook my head to clear the vapors clouding my mind. "I still don't understand."

"No one truly understands magic. And it's a good thing, too. Can you imagine the potential for power if someone did? They might rule the world itself!"

"And that would be a bad thing?" I muttered wryly. The concept sounded rather appealing to me. So long as I were the one in charge, of course. I would hate someone else having that much power over me.

"Of course it would be a bad thing!" Mercy insisted. "I'm sure you've heard the famous saying *'absolute power doth absolutely corrupt'?* What person is equipped to wield or cope with so much power? It would be to their ruination, as well as everyone else's."

"If you say so," I agreed mildly, not prepared to argue the point. It would never happen anyway, so what was to quarrel about? If I did have absolute power, my first act would be to erect impenetrable barriers around my campsite, so Princess Mercy couldn't pester me anymore. Sadly, it appeared there would be no getting rid of this girl unless I bound her hand and foot, shoved her into a burlap sack, and dropped her into the river. Somehow, despite all she'd done to vex me, I could no more harm such an innocent than I could stomp a litter of kittens to death.

Coward, chided my crueler side.

I didn't bother to dispute. Give me thirty knights to face and a piece of ground over which to fight: I would charge boldly and do battle to the death. But against a pair of large blue eyes, a sassy tongue, and a sweet face I shrank like a whipped pup.

Pathetic. Truly pathetic.

"But where did you learn this skill?" I wanted to know. "Who would teach a princess about manipulating the forces of magic?"

Mercy shrugged. "Oh, the Curator, of course. He lives in the forest next to this one. I'm surprised you haven't made his acquaintance by now."

"The Curator?"

My mind leapt back to the cantankerous old man I'd met by the edge of the brook, the one who had tried to kill me.

"Yes, the Curator. He knows a great deal about

magic, for all that he's a veritable hermit and never leaves his hut. I met him long ago, as a child. We've been friends for years. Sometimes I bring him baskets of food or baked treats. He likes Cook's rosemary scones the best. In return, he has taught me a thing or two about dealing with magic, such as building fires like this one." She nodded at the cheery blaze. "I've not seen him in quite some time. I should visit him again."

I must admit I was having difficulties reconciling the gaffer I had met with a hermit befriended by talkative Mercy. I'd no reason to doubt her word, however, especially when she spoke again.

"He has a wolf that is green with red eyes. Very evil looking, but he and I are also old friends. The Curator claims he has never seen the wolf take to anyone the way he does to me."

Uh oh. *Gindlon's toes!* What would she think to discover I had not only made the Curator's acquaintance, but also that of his wolf? What would she think to know that I had killed her friend? How did one befriend a wolf anyway? How did one befriend the Curator? For some reason, I was not surprised to find out, if anyone had, it was this young woman.

Just as she seeks to befriend you.

The correlation between kind Mercy befriending the Curator, his evil looking wolf, and myself were too uncomfortable to consider. In order to change the subject, I leapt to my feet and announced that I was going to fetch wood to feed her fire.

Thankfully, Mercy seemed to put our conversation out of her mind. While I was gone, she commenced breakfast, whipping up a dish of eggs flavored with the tiny red mushrooms growing beneath nearly every tree in the forest, and accompanied by bread spread with a paste she produced by mixing water, ground bark from the local *uliela tree*, and a single duck egg. She admitted none of the ingredients until after I'd eaten, then had a good laugh at my disgusted expression.

"I cannot believe you would feed me that," I grumbled, praying fervently that such culinary oddities wouldn't turn on me.

"Don't be foolish. It will do you no harm, and it was delicious, wasn't it? Those are the same ingredients famous chefs use. They always cook with strange ingredients. Anyway, you love my cooking, no matter the elements. Just admit it."

I couldn't deny it, but I did say, "After this, please don't tell me what you put in your concoctions. I'd rather not know."

Laughing at my "weak stomach," as she called it, she agreed.

We worked together to clear away the breakfast mess. Her former downcast mood forgotten, Mercy of Merris chattered about one subject after another until my ears were ringing and my brain stuffed full. I was beginning to wonder if her father drove her out of the castle every day to be rid of the sound of her voice.

She'd returned my red tunic, which she had taken yesterday. After using it again as an apron while cooking, she rinsed it out in the nearby spring, scrubbed off the spots of grease and food, then hung the garment from a nearby tree branch to dry.

"I cannot believe you would use my tunic, uninvited, as a cooking apron," I grouched when she returned to plop down unceremoniously at my side.

"You do not believe a great many things," she reproved.

I'd nothing to say to that, because it was true. For a while we sat in silence. Only for a while, though, because Lady Mercy was not one to sit still or silent for long.

The next thing I knew, she'd slapped my forearm to garner my attention. "I've an idea!" she announced, bounding to her feet.

I rolled my eyes, still focusing on the lump in my stomach, into which my breakfast had balled as soon as she confessed what she'd fed me. *Is this going to stay down?* was what I'd been thinking, but clearly the princess's line of thought had been far afield.

"I want to ride your horse," she said, gathering her skirts in one hand and striding off to where Stalker grazed beneath a giant oak spreading its boughs toward a sapphire sky.

"What? Oh no—oh no, you don't!" Instantly, I was on my feet and giving chase. "Have you lost your mind, woman?" I barked, swinging around to put myself between princess and warhorse. Stalker didn't so much as glance up from his grazing, but continued ripping up tufts of green grass with long, strong teeth.

"You never, *never* mount a strange horse without its owner's permission. And that goes double for a warhorse. What were you thinking? Such an animal is just as apt to kill you as allow you to touch him."

She gave me a patronizing look. "He and I are friends," she pointed out. "Stalker would never harm me."

"Be that as it may," I spoke firmly. "Stalker is no child's mount, but a knight's destrier. He is trained to carry his rider onto fields of combat, and even to assist in battle. He—"

"I know, I know," she cut in, holding up a hand. "He is trained to kill. He has killed, many a time."

"Yes, he has," I started to say, but she went on before I could.

"Spare me the lecture on his murderous adventures. I know he would never harm me, and you know it as well. You're just determined to be selfish. If you don't wish me to ride him, all you need do is say so. You shouldn't hide behind poor excuses to justify your pettiness."

"I don't wish you to ride him," I said through gritted teeth, "but it has nothing to do with pettiness. It's your safety that concerns me. I'm a guest in your father's kingdom. How would he feel if I permitted this and you came to harm?"

"My safety?" The look she gave me was mocking indeed. "I am amazed that it concerns you at all!"

With that, she whirled with a swish of her royal skirts and stomped back over to the campfire where she sank down in the exact same spot as before.

Heaving a quiet sigh of both reluctance and relief, I gave Stalker a friendly slap on the rump and followed.

CHAPTER SIX
Of Rumors and Games

Now I'd done it. I had made the princess angry by refusing to let her ride Stalker. Well, and what should I have done in that situation? Sit idly by while she climbed onto my warhorse, fell off a moment later, and broke her neck? How would I explain that to her father, the king? Bringing King Merl his daughter's limp, lifeless body was not exactly how I envisioned being introduced to the ruler of Merris.

Princess Mercy was as full of flighty ideas as a chicken. Or...or was she really as bad as I supposed?

Unbeknownst to me, I was about to learn some startling truths from this maiden, truths that continued changing my perceptions of who and what she was.

When I went back to my campfire and seated myself beside Merris's frustrating princess, she turned her nose up in the air and refused to speak.

Nor had I any remarks to offer. For a time, we sat in silence, save for the pleasant resonances of nature. Idly, I picked up a stick and began to poke at the fire. Just as I did, she slapped my forearm again to capture my attention.

"Play Questions with me," ordered the princess when I dropped the stick and shifted her way.

"Questions? What is that?" I asked suspiciously, mistrustful of any ideas she might present.

"I ask ten questions, which you must answer truthfully, and then you do the same to me."

"That's a bad idea."

"No, it's not. It is a good way to get to know one another."

I cocked an eyebrow, trying to imitate her condescending cocked eyebrow of the day before. "We don't know one another?"

"Not as well as we could," she pointed out. "And one of the best ways for friends to deepen their acquaintance is to play Questions. Come, Sir Buck, you aren't afraid of playing a game with me, surely?"

She was testing me, I could tell. Questioning my bravery, my manhood. I would not let her have the upper hand in this.

"I fear nothing," I proclaimed valiantly, "least of all anything you might devise."

"Wonderful!" She clapped her hands together, apparently having forgotten or forgiven the forbidden riding incident. "Then let us play. I shall go first."

Most of her questions were frivolous inquiries—what colors I liked, what foods, what breeds of horse, what manner of weapons: sword, spear, lance, mace, etc. It was not until she reached question number nine that she finally delved deeper.

Knight's Rebirth

"Why do you live as an itinerant knight, traveling from tournament to tournament, instead of settling down, marrying, and building a castle of your own? I know you have sufficient funds," she added. "It's no secret you've won many purses of gold at the events where you were champion."

"What?" I sputtered, knocked for six that she'd heard the outlandish rumors accompanying my reputation as a tournament-winning knight. And there were scores of them. A few were true or at least grounded in truth. Others were so silly as to border on absurdity.

One of the wilder legends claimed that I left my money in the care of a fire-breathing dragon, for dragons (as everyone knows) love nothing better than hoarding treasure in their caves. Another tale claimed I'd invested my riches in a garment making facility, using the saddlebags crammed with silks and laces and satins to supply the cloth for women's frocks. Still another maintained that I owned four castles in four different realms, wherein my four different wives were kept, one for each season of the year.

Some alleged that I was the High King's illegitimate child, who, though he loved, he could not publicly acknowledge. Never mind that his majesty High King Delmont was less than fifteen years my senior; some swore he rigged all events I entered, so that his favorite child would win. Yet another tale, cousin to this one but slightly different, swore that I was not Delmont's son but his brother, and that was why he rigged events to ensure my victory.

Ridiculous rumors, one and all. I killed dragons; I didn't use them for bankers. I distributed the favors to poor dressmakers needing fabric, or street children who could hawk them for money. Above all, I certainly had no secret castles or hidden wives. And the High King was definitely neither my father nor my brother. Such malarkey. Would not High Queen Teressa have been amazed to hear her husband claim me as his son? Would not the old Queen Mother, Broomalda, have rolled over in her grave to hear him own me as a brother? Not to mention, the notion that I needed events to be rigged in my favor in order to be named champion was just insulting.

"I live as an itinerant knight because that's the life I enjoy," I told my companion flatly. I then proceeded to run through the most popular tales about me and name them as lies. "You should not believe everything you hear," I admonished when I was done. "It saves you from falling prey to many an exaggeration or falsehood."

"I never said I believed the tales," she countered. "I merely mentioned your feats in the lists were no secret." She hesitated. "But, now that we've opened the subject, what *do* you do with all the money you've won, if a dragon does not guard it?"

Gindlon preserve us, I swore, unable to conceive of even Mercy believing such rubbish.

"A real banker keeps what I don't carry for traveling expenses," I informed her sardonically. "What else would I do with it? I certainly wouldn't trust it to a greedy serpent. One day, when I am too old and decrepit to fight, I'll build a spacious castle and marry a desperate, middle-aged widow who'll be content to look after my estate without plaguing me endlessly for new gowns and expensive shoes."

"And here I was under the impression you

planned to live out your last days in a gusty old cottage as a cranky, wheezing gaffer, lonely and alone," she replied innocently.

I threw her a cutting glare. "Oh, you think yourself so clever..."

She dissolved into laughter. "What a fine jest. You, the mighty Sir Buckhunter Dornley, a grouchy old grandfather stumbling about on a cane. Yes, yes I can see it now."

"Not funny," I growled, crossing my arms threateningly over my chest.

"Yes, it is."

Before I could offer a piercing comeback, she jumped in with her tenth question.

"So, how did you become a traveling knight? What would make a man choose such a career?"

My anger fled as I considered the inquiry. In the end, I told her what I'd never told another living soul. Why, I don't know, except as scatty as Mercy of Merris seemed, deep in my heart I believed her capable of keeping a secret.

"I was born the second son of an affluent Earl," I began slowly. "Growing up, my elder brother was Father's pride and joy, while the man had little use for me. Once I reached my majority, Father cast me out of his manse—afraid, I suppose, that I'd attempt to usurp Rikkard's place as heir.

"He was always sickly and cross, was Rikkard, while I tended to be the outdoorsy sort, forever getting into scrapes with the pages and stable lads. Rikkard did not like the outdoors, fighting, or any sort of manly pursuits. He preferred writing dour poetry and painting gloomy pictures. Oh, and he was always and ever seeking ways to put me down in

Father's eyes. I suppose I was about thirteen when he began whispering that I planned to assume his position as heir.

"Of course I'd no intention of doing anything of the sort," I hastened to clarify, "but that became both Father and Rikkard's belief, possibly augmented by the fact that, had I wanted to challenge Rikkard for the birthright, I would have prevailed. It was at that age I went to train with the High King's champion, and by the time I returned, having earned my knighthood, Rikkard had filled Father's ears with so much poison that I was given no more inheritance than a few golden coins, a fine sword with which to defend my life, and my destrier, Stalker. Add to that excellent training and innate determination, and I had all I needed to survive."

"And prosper," she agreed thoughtfully, looking me up and down. "From such humble beginnings, you've certainly done well for yourself. You are, undoubtedly, the most famous and feared knight in the land. Your reputation precedes you wherever you go. Kings and noblemen alike would pay any amount for your services, fathers offer any dowry to have you as a son-in-law."

"And how would you know that? I've told you nothing of the sort."

A funny sort of smile lifted one corner of her mouth. "Oh, Sir Buck, think me a fool but do not think me naive. Naturally, I hear things. My father is one of many kings desirous of engaging your services. Sir Buckhunter Dornley is an unusual name, and it is a name bandied about court between noble men and women alike."

I regarded her skeptically, a light dawning in my

head. "How long have you known?"

"All along," she confessed, unashamed of the fact. "I doubt there are two Sir Buckhunter Dornleys in the world. I'm uncertain the world could handle two of you, to tell the truth."

Before I could protest that little gibe, she went on. "Furthermore, your emblem—" she nodded towards my shield, propped against an adjacent tree "—of four purple dragons with their necks intertwined is distinct. As soon as I saw it, I knew."

"Then why not admit it?" I cried, throwing my hands in the air. "Why maintain the charade of treating me like I was a nobody?"

She regarded me steadily, evenly. "Because famous people are far more likely to be themselves when they presume others are ignorant of their identity. I wanted to see what manner of man you were."

"And have you seen?"

Suddenly, I was anxious to know. Why, I couldn't say. It wasn't as if I'd ever sought to recommend myself to her. Why should I care what she thought of me?

"A good one," she responded, tossing her hair back over one shoulder and smiling. "An irritable, but good one. By now, a lesser man would have surely carried through on his threats of tossing me off a cliff. But you have forborne, and for this I am forever in your debt." Placing both hands together, she offered me a mock bow.

I shook my head at her folly, restraining a grin. "I may be a good man, but, were I you, I would press me no further. You've come dreadfully close to causing my patience to snap."

"I'm not afraid. You would never harm me."

"Are you certain of that?" Placing a palm on the log between us, I leaned close, peering deeply into her eyes.

Giggling, she pushed me away. "Naturally, 'else I would not risk being alone with you."

"How peculiar. I was under the impression that you made it a practice to torment men alone."

"No, although each day I live I do make a practice of helping someone or brightening their day."

"And why is that?"

I sat back, giving her room. Giving *me* room, because I needed it. She was far from a celebrated beauty, but she was a pretty girl, even if rather maddening. I was afraid this newfound physical attraction would require little to encourage it. Which I wasn't about to do.

"Because," she replied, serious all of a sudden. Her gaze fell to her hands, which were folded in her lap. Her thumbs, however, twiddled nervously. "I've no idea how much time is given me to live. I would use my life as a means of aiding or giving happiness to others. It's the best way I've found to make a difference, to make my existence count for something."

"That is a strange philosophy for someone so young," I observed, but Mercy disagreed.

"I don't think so. If more people felt the same, don't you think this world would be a much better place?" She left off studying her fingers to gaze up earnestly into my face. "Don't you think selfishness is one of the greatest wrongs in the world? I do. I believe nothing causes more unhappiness, with the possible exception of pride. Wouldn't you agree, Sir Buck?"

"I suppose," I concurred carefully.

What was she driving at? Was this little sermonette aimed at me? I...well, maybe I was a tad proud. And selfish. Oh very well, perhaps I was more than just a tad. But had I not redeemed myself in some measure by putting up with Mercy for the past few days? As she herself had claimed, a lesser man would have tossed her off a cliff by now, which I hadn't. Surely that must count for something.

No matter what arguments I made to myself, I still squirmed uncomfortably, feeling as if the finger of doom were pointing directly at me. The feeling only worsened when Mercy added,

"I've brightened your days, haven't I? I've tried to, anyway. From the first time I saw you, sleeping alone in the forest with no company besides your horse, I knew how lonely you must be. And when we talked, and you were so harsh and grumpy and bitter, I thought, *Here is a man with much anger at the world around him. Never mind his fame and fortune and all the women swooning over his feats in the lists, he needs a friend. A real friend, besides his horse.* So I have tried to be that friend to you. I hope I have succeeded, and the past few days have been a little less lonesome for you."

She had shocked me many times in the course of our brief acquaintance, but nothing struck me like those words. I was so dumbfounded that my protest of, "I am neither lonely nor angry at the world around me," came out as more of a half-hearted mumble than a vigorous protest.

Until I'd met her, met someone who insisted on befriending those who held the world at arm's length—myself, the Curator—I never would have admitted that perhaps beneath the gilt and trappings of a famous knight, there was a part of me still bitter over my family's betrayal. Rikkard, for accusing me of crimes I'd never committed. Father, for believing and backing him. Mother, even though I'd been loved by her, for not having the fortitude to side with me. Maybe knowing those who should have been my first supporters but had betrayed me helped account for my distaste for a domestic life. After all, if my original family cared so little for me, who was to say a wife, children, might not treat me the same in the end?

All that aside, it was more than a little astonishing that this young woman who presented such a carefree demeanor could have read me well enough in only a handful of meetings to sense any of this. It was astounding that she had put so much work into trying to befriend a snappish stranger. It was even more astounding that she cared.

I could not remember the last time anyone had cared about me, my fame and fortune aside. As for those, Mercy cared about neither. Her father did, as she'd admitted already, but not her.

If she noticed how much her admission had thrown me, and how brittle was my objection, she kindly let it go, refusing to pounce on my moment of weakness. Instead, she said, "If we are only to be friends for a short time, at least we are friends for now."

There was a hint of sadness in her eyes. I caught it, and asked, "Why only a short time?"

She bit her lip and gave her shoulders a little shrug. "I suppose because you are not going to stay here forever, yes? Someday you will have to move on to the next tournament or dragon hunt, or whatever it is that you do."

"Ah."

Her explanation made sense, but it did not account for the sorrow in her gaze. Was she saddened by the thought of me leaving? Or by something else?

"Well," she sighed, peering upwards at the sky. "The morn passes swiftly. I'd best return to the castle, lest they begin to search for me."

"Wait," I protested, thrusting out a hand to restrain her. "We didn't finish playing Questions."

"I thought you hated playing Questions," she rebuked. "Now you want to finish the game?"

"Is it not unfair for you to ask me ten questions, and I not be able to ask you any?"

"Very well, then—ask me a question. But only one, mind you. Unlike some folks, I haven't all day to loiter in the woods."

"Curious...one would never know that by your numerous visits."

After debating a bit on what one question to ask, I inquired about her cooking, for it was a side of her that truly puzzled me.

"Why do you cook? I was of the opinion princesses learned to dance gracefully, walk with books on their heads, stitch tapestries, ride placid mares, dress in all the latest fashions, and snare handsome, wealthy princes for husbands. I didn't know they were schooled in the culinary arts, as well."

"They usually aren't," she disclosed. "But I tired quickly of those other pursuits. I'm no normal princess, I fear. I cannot dance gracefully, the book ever and always fell from my head, my thread knotted and tangled, and I prefer plain, sturdy clothing to whatever frills and frippery happen to be in fashion.

Above all, I have no interest in snaring a prince for a husband.

"I can ride, though," she went on cheerily. "And not just placid mares. No matter what you may think, Sir Knight, I would have gotten along splendidly with Stalker. I love nothing better than a gallop on a fiery steed."

I chose to ignore that comment. "And the cooking?"

She shrugged. "It's a pleasant pastime. I enjoyed learning to cook, I enjoy creating new dishes I've never tried before, and I enjoy it when others enjoy the fruits of my labors. I love mixing this with that, seeing what flavors combine well and what don't. I love creating dishes as beautiful in appearance as they are satisfying to the palate. Had I the time, I would visit some of the realm's famous cooking schools and meet the chefs I admire. I would love the opportunity to learn from them, instead of merely from their cookbooks."

"Perhaps if you would stop pestering people in your father's woods, you would have the time to meet these chefs of yours," I goaded her.

She responded with a mock glare. "Very funny, Sir Knight. Very funny."

CHAPTER SEVEN
Of Silence and Love

How can someone so insufferable turn into someone you miss so terribly? I've no idea, but that became the case with me.

Mercy.

Mercy and her chattering.

Something that initially made me want to cover my ears and run the other way became something and someone I could not live without.

Maybe it's like the tale of the old widow woman, whose husband of fifty-odd years used to snore so terribly. She hated that snoring while he lived, and complained and grouched about it to anyone who would listen. "What I wouldn't give for one night of unbroken sleep!" was her refrain. When he was taken ill and died she came to realize how much she missed his snoring—that same snoring which had formerly been such an aggravation.

"What I wouldn't give to hear his dear old snoring just one more time!" she now moans.

Maybe that was the case with me. Me and my princess's lively chatter.

Mercy left soon after that...and I had never heard such quiet. Strange how people can quickly become accustomed, or even attached, to something. At first, Mercy's incessant prattle had driven me half mad. Now the silence of the forest, unbroken by her cheery chatter, was enough to make me doubt my sanity.

"Where did all this quiet come from?" I asked Stalker, who flicked a fly off his left ear and continued nibbling at a tasty green clump. "Why haven't I noticed it before?"

Although I tried to fill in the remaining hours of the day with this and that, I soon found nothing could entertain me or hold my interest for long. I tried talking to Stalker, but horses are pretty poor conversationalists. I even tried talking to myself, but remembered the princess's jest about folks thinking others peculiar who talk to themselves and broke off.

In desperation, I started to sing a few bawdy tavern songs such as all traveling men know, but wound up not being able to finish a single one. All I could see in my mind's eye was Mercy, reproach on her face, telling me I knew better and I ought to be ashamed of myself.

Oddly enough, I was. So I sang no more bawdy tavern songs.

That night I retired early, went straight to bed, and fell fast asleep. My sleep was hardly peaceful, for dreams of Merris's princess plagued me all night long. In my dreams she babbled incessantly, scarcely pausing to draw breath. It was so bad I stormed to the edge of a cliff, and gave serious thought to either jumping off or throwing her off.

Actually, there was a cliff not very far away. Not a soaring cliff, but a bluff overlooking a forest ravine, the bottom of which was scattered with boulders. Awakening, I went for a walk to clear my mind of dreams and thoughts of Merris's princess. I was strolling along the edge of the ravine, wading through flowering gorse brush higher than my waist that grew right up to the cliff's brink. At the summit, where the gorse finally cleared because of the rockiness of the ground, I stopped to catch my breath and gaze down at the view, studying the ravine as it meandered along until it was lost in the shadows of distant, overhanging trees.

A small pool lay at the bottom of the ravine floor. I was leaning over, considering how I might climb down to the bottom for a closer look, both as a diversion and some good exercise, when I heard a sudden rustling. I barely had time to turn my head to seek the source of the sound, when I was hit in the side by a small, solid object, which attempted to push me back from the cliff's edge.

"Buck, don't!" someone cried.

It was Mercy. I should've known. Her efforts to knock me back, however well-intentioned, did little more than make me stumble.

"Gindlon's bones, woman, what are you doing?" I squawked, catching her with an arm about the waist and, in a single movement, swinging her around as I fumbled back from the verge, lest her shove and my stumble accidentally send us both tumbling over the cliff rather than away from it, as she surely intended.

Soon as I set her down and released her, she stepped back, her cheeks red with exertion and her hair mussed.

"What am I doing? What are you doing?" she snapped, hands on her hips, looking fierce. "Are you trying to kill yourself? Why would you do that?"

"Kill myself?" I echoed. Discombobulated, I stared down at her, wondering what wild notions could be running through her head. "Why would I be attempting to kill myself?" I finally gathered the wits to ask. "And what did you think to gain by acting as you did? You are not strong enough to prevent me if I had intended to jump. You would have simply wound up going over the edge with me."

"Well, I had to try!" her face was even redder, whether from embarrassment or anger or both, I couldn't tell. "I know there is loneliness in your life, but I'm your friend now, and I would not let even a big oaf such as you jump to their doom without trying to save him."

"You would risk your life to save this big oaf? Why, Mercy of Merris, I did not know you cared."

Her blue eyes narrowed to a squint. "I don't. No more than I do for any other person. But, however grumpy and sour you may be, you are a human life, and I think that is worth saving."

Before I could respond, she turned about and started fighting her way through the gorse, head held high.

"Mercy…"

Already I felt sorry for teasing her. She had acted impulsively on a completely incorrect diagnosis, but she had acted. She'd acted to save my life, never mind my oftentimes grumpy, sour demeanor toward her.

She had potentially put her own life at risk to save mine. She'd said my life was worth saving, and she meant it. Unfounded as her fears had been, she'd done her best to protect me.

Her—protect me.

I was oddly touched.

"Mercy..."

My legs were longer than hers, and it was easier for me to wade through the shrubs in trousers than her in her skirts. I caught up to her in a few strides, grasping her gently by the arm.

"Wait, Princess."

She halted reluctantly, but would not face me.

"Why, so you can mock me again for trying to save your life?"

My life needed no saving, I almost remonstrated. Instead, that soft place in my heart, oddly touched by her deed, kept my mouth closed.

"I have no reason to kill myself," I said as patiently as I could. "I was in no danger. However, you did not know that, and I suppose my position could have looked precarious," I admitted.

"It did," she snapped, turning to face me. "I'm not the ninny you suppose I am. I like to pester and tease you because you respond so viciously, but I am not a fool, whatever you may think. I truly feared you were in danger. I do not go throwing myself at men for a lark."

This man rather enjoyed you throwing yourself at him.

That was a strange thought. I was used to maidens throwing themselves at me, but I had certainly never enjoyed it. I'd always fled them. Mercy, though...

Stop it, fool! I scolded myself, cutting off that line of thought before it could advance any further.

To Mercy, I said, "I am sure you do not. And I thank you for doing what you did…although you were wrong."

The last part I said in a way meant to provoke her bantering side. It worked. The irritation faded as she stuck her nose with the little bump in the air.

"Well, that does not happen often, I will have you know."

"Undoubtedly," I chuckled, shaking my head. Clasping her elbow, I guided her back towards my camp, doing my best to shove the gorse out of her path with my free hand.

"It doesn't," she asserted.

"I believe you."

"You don't sound as if you believe me."

"Take my words as you will," I said, as we finally broke free of the brush and entered a more level place, "but also know that while I truly did not need saving, I do value your attempt to rescue me."

She turned to look up at me. A gentle breeze stirred her mussed hair, filling me with a wild notion to reach up and tuck the stray wisps behind her ear. I was not usually given to wild notions, not like the princess standing before me. Where had it come from?

I restrained the impulse as she smiled sweetly and said, "Well, this world could always use a few less cross words in it, but I suppose it could always use more champions too. So in order to have the champion, we must also put up with the cross words, yes?"

Her assessment made me feel cross.

"I am not always cross," I said.

"You seem to be with me."

"That is because you make me cross."

I could see the glint in her eye, and knew she was deliberately provoking me, trying to reclaim the upper hand. It was working. How did she always manage that?

Before I could puzzle out the mystery, she laid a hand on my arm. "I must get back to the palace. Duty calls, and I could only afford a short visit today. Please be careful, and take no tumbles off cliffs while I am not present to catch you."

"I was not—" *about to take a tumble off the cliff!* I started to say, but then sighed and surrendered. What was the use? What was ever the use of arguing with Mercy of Merris? Somehow, she always gained the advantage, which so frustrated me that I nearly forgot my softer feelings toward her earlier.

Nearly. But not entirely.

That night, I dreamt that I awoke and stirred from my tent, only to see her bending over my campfire, singing annoyingly happy songs while manipulating magical flames and cooking me a meal comprised of vile ingredients. The dreams were as bad as reality, and I awoke in a foul humor.

She'd best not come by today. On my knees, I gazed at the bloodshot eyes and surly countenance reflected in the clear water of the stream. *She'll not like what she finds.*

That was my first peevish thought. Come an hour later, when I had breakfasted and my humor was altered for the better, I caught my ears straining for the sounds of feet approaching through the trees.

Where is she? I kept thinking. *She is never this*

late.

Another hour passed, then two. By now, the horrid mood had returned—worsened, even. This time, much to my chagrin, Princess Mercy was the cause of it. Or rather, her absence was the cause of it.

Where is she? Where in Gindlon's name is she? I wondered over and over again. No day had ever been so long, so boring. So...quiet.

That night I dreamed of her again, and this time she had two towheaded younglings clinging to her skirts whilst she cooked something that smelled delicious in a large, comfortable kitchen. Seated upon a padded bench, I watched them with pride, feeling as contended as a man can feel. Something small and warm filled my arms, and when I glanced down I saw a baby nestled there. A wee elfish girl, with Mercy's brown-blonde hair and my dark grey eyes.

What in Gindlon's name?

I wakened with a start, breathing hard, as if I'd just battled three dragons at once. Me? Married to Mercy? With children between us? Horrible notion, terrible idea!

Or was it?

Flopping back onto my bedroll, I rolled over on my side, squeezing my eyes tightly shut. *No,* I rebuked myself sternly. *No, I won't think of her like that. She would drive me mad, and I've no wish to be a father. Nor a husband, either.*

But maybe that dream was trying to tell me something, something my heart was leaning towards, even if my head refused to concede.

During the next few days, days in which Mercy continued to remain absent, I found I simply could not forget that dream. Neither the dream nor the fact of her trying, as she thought, to save my life. Telling me my life was worth saving. Braving my gruffness to make herself my friend. No matter what I gave myself to—sword practice, galloping Stalker, washing my clothes, scrubbing my dishes, hunting a fine stag— these things insisted on coming to mind.

Despite my mental confusion, those days passed in a steady, boring quietness that ate at my soul. I could have left, could have moved on, but...I didn't want to. Not without seeing Mercy again. By the time I rolled into my lonely bed at the end of another long, silent day, I realized something profound: I missed her.

Despite my initial testiness over everything she'd said and done, somehow her quirky mannerisms had wormed their way deep into my heart. I *did* miss her, and hadn't been able to expel her from my mind for several consecutive days. No other woman, no matter her beauty, rank, or wealth, had ever accomplished this. Which must mean, much as I loathed to admit it, that this went far deeper than merely missing her.

I drew in a deep breath, releasing it in a slow whoosh of air as I whispered the truth to myself:

"Maybe I...I love her."

There it was. *I loved her.* Gindlon's ghost only knew how, but it seemed I'd somehow fallen in love with a woman for whom I'd never expected to feel anything except hatred...or at least mild detestation. Certainly, I'd not counted on being attracted to her (which I was), wanting her (which I did), or loving her.

Mercy of Merris, I groaned, throwing a forearm across my face. *What have you done to me?*

That was the longest night of my life. I missed

her. I'd missed her for days! I couldn't help thinking of her, imagining her as my wife. Loving a woman had turned me into fancy's fool.

Winning tournaments would be nothing compared to winning the heart and hand of Mercy of Merris, and before the sun peeked its round, orange face over the emerald tops of the trees, I was up and stirring about. A plan had formed during the nighttime hours, and I was ready to act. If she would not come to me, I must go to her. It was high time Sir Buckhunter Dornley ceased fleeing the bonds of matrimony, and entered them instead.

That day she came, and I'd never been so happy to see anyone. When she arrived I was shaving, preparing myself to leave for the palace and seek an audience with its princess. I was kneeling beside a calm part of the stream, using it as my mirror, when behind me I heard Mercy's trademark light, quick footsteps. I froze, hardly daring to breathe. I was dying to see her, but at the same time foolishly feared that somehow, someway, it would not be her at all. And then a woman's hand settled on my shoulder. Mercy's voice, which I had been longing to hear, offered a gentle, "Good morning, Buck."

For a long moment I remained where I was, simply enjoying the wonder of her presence.

"And to you, Mercy," I answered at last, angling my head to stare up into her face.

How had I once considered her only mildly

pretty? She was truly beautiful. The late morning sun created a halo of her dark blonde hair, and her blue eyes sparkled like sapphires.

Laying aside my razor, I dashed a handful of water over my face before rising to my feet, smiling down at her. The top of her head did not quite reach my shoulder, yet were I to take her in my arms, I knew she'd be more than enough to fill them forever.

"Well, this is not quite the reaction I expected," she teased. "Usually when we first meet you are in a terrible temper that I must coax out of you."

"Mercy..."

I was in no mood to jest. The words I wanted to say bubbled up from deep within, overcrowding my tongue and fogging my brain. More than anything I wanted to confess my love and ask her to marry me. How did a man state this?

In the end, I simply opened my mouth. What came out was, "Where have you been these past few days?"

Not the most persuasive or romantic of comments, but it was something I had pondered often enough.

She grinned. "Why? Did you miss me?"

Clearly she expected some snappish, rude reply like I would have given before. She did not get that today.

"Yes," I returned honestly. "I missed you a great deal."

My confession took her aback, I could tell. When she hesitated, visibly reeling from shock, I decided to take my chances. Stepping forward, I caught her by the waist and drew her close.

"Yes, Mercy, I missed you. I missed you more

than you could ever know. I dreamed of you these nights you've been away. I thought of you ceaselessly."

The emotions racing across her face appeared and vanished so swiftly it was difficult to tell what she was thinking. Amazement, fear, joy, awe...

Taking a deep breath, I fortified myself and plunged on.

"Mercy, never again do I wish to be separated from you, for I—I love you." Her jaw dropped. Was that a good sign? "Mercy, I know I'm unworthy, but I would be the happiest man in the world if you would marry me." I drew her even closer, wrapping my arms about her. "I love you, sweet girl. Say you'll be my wife."

She braced herself with her hands against my chest, scowling up into my face. "Buckhunter Dornley, is this a jest? Or have you gone mad?"

Oddly enough, I found the question funny. "Yes," I laughed. Transferring my grip to her waist, I swept her easily off her feet, bringing her face level with mine. "Yes, I am mad...mad about you, my love."

She rolled her eyes, giving me a swat on the shoulder. "Buck, you fool, put me down!"

"Not until you promise to marry me," I warned.

"Buck!"

"Yes, my love?"

She cupped my neck between her palms, touching her nose to mine. "Put...me...down, you silly man. I cannot think what has gotten into you."

"*You* have gotten into me," I told her, all playfulness fading. "You and you alone, Mercy of Merris. How you did it or what enchantments you used, I neither know nor care." Slowly, I lowered her

Knight's Rebirth

to the ground, although I kept my hands on her waist. "Marry me, Mercy. Please. I love you."

For the first time, she realized this was no joke and I was perfectly serious. "Buck," she faltered, all traces of lightheartedness fleeing. "You don't know what you're asking."

"How can you say that? I do know. I want you for my wife. Is that so wrong? I know I could never be worthy of you, but I would love you and care for you and be faithful to you—"

To my horror, tears flooded her eyes, and they were not tears of joy. Her face went pale. "No, Buck, I can't!" she whispered, straining against my grip. Panic flooded her features.

"Mercy—"

"No, Buck. I can't—I simply can't! Please let me go. You don't understand, you really don't."

"Don't understand what?" I asked, but somehow she'd loosened my hands. Before I knew quite what was happening, she'd torn loose and dashed a safe distance away.

"Buck, how can I say this? You must forget this madcap scheme. You must forget me." Her hands twisted in her skirts. "I never intended this outcome. I never meant to make you love me. I am so sorry. Please forgive me for—" She stopped, shaking her head. "I am so sorry. Please go. Leave my father's lands, and go. You must go."

Before I could say anything else, she'd whirled to flee, not walking but running away, leaving me alone in a state of complete bewilderment.

It didn't last long.

Never let it be said that Sir Buckhunter Dornley was a man easily dissuaded. Mercy cared for me; I knew she did. A dismissal of my first proposal meant nothing. Clearly, there was some underlying reason for her staunch rejections and flight, a reason I meant to uncover. Uncover, set to rights, and afterward claim Mercy of Merris as my own, if she would have me.

CHAPTER EIGHT
Of Fairytale Palaces and Elder Sisters

Now this was a pretty pass. For years the most famous knight in Gindsland had been sought after by a host of eligible young ladies who would have given their eyeteeth to wed him.

For equally as many years, this same knight had used every means within his power to avoid them. But now, in only a week he had fallen hard and fast for the one woman in the entire empire who'd not only refused his offer of marriage, but said she never meant to make him love her and asked him to go.

I had no idea why, but I knew it must be something dreadfully serious. The idea of Mercy not returning my love never occurred to me. What woman wouldn't love me?

I'm sure you recognize my vast conceit. Still, you must allow that by this point I'd already changed a great deal. What it would take for me to be completely rebirthed, however, you must keep reading to find out.

After making swift work of disassembling my campsite, I was on my way. Leaving the forest, I chanced upon a narrow, winding trail, which eventually led me into the heart of a small village. There, I asked directions for the main road that would lead me to the capital city and the king's palace.

"When ye come to the crossroads a mile yonder," replied the old villager, leaning heavily upon a cane, "which be called Hanging Crossroads—aye, and it be called that 'cause it be where they hang con-victed murderers."

His accent placed an unusual pause between *con* and *victed*.

"Ye wouldn't happen to be one of them con-victed murderers, would ye, man?" he inquired rather hopefully.

Doing my best to remain patient, I assured him I was not.

"Fiddle," he said. "We ain't had nary a good hanging at the Crossroads since…since…" Lost in thought, he gave his shaggy grey head a good scratching, as if that alone would speed up the mental processes.

I felt my impatience growing. "The road to the palace, please," I reminded him rather sharply.

"Eh? Oh, aye, the road to the palace. Well, when ye come to Hanging Crossroads," he went on, pointing a trembly finger due south, "ye'll take the road what branches off to the right. That'll put ye on the main highway. The palace be but a mile beyond."

Pausing, he looked me up and down, taking in my size, physique, weapons, and steed. "Aye, ye look too fine to be a con-victed murderer. So, if ye ain't, that means ye've business with the king?"

"Possibly," I evaded, unwilling to be drawn into further conversation that would delay my plans. "My thanks for your help, grandfather." I flipped him a gold coin which he caught easily, displaying an agility for which I'd never have given him credit.

"A good day to ye, sir!" he called after me, waving a bony arm. "A good day and good luck. Dinna forget now: Hanging Crossroads. It be where they—"

"I know, I know," I shouted, kicking Stalker into a trot. To myself, I grumbled, "With any luck, I'll not wind up there as your evening entertainment!"

The short distance to the palace flew by with memories of Mercy to keep me company. As I rode, thinking of her, I wondered how long it took her to journey from her castle to my former campsite.

Must be a shortcut through the trees, I decided, for I doubted she'd have taken the trouble to walk this distance every day just to visit me. Although I could have searched for it, I chose to follow the old villager's advice and keep to the roads, saving myself some time.

Mercy's home, when I finally glimpsed it, was charming. It was a castle from a fairy story. Emerging from a sea of bright green leaves, its graceful towers and spires could be seen from some distance off. A winding lane of crushed white shells branched off from the main highway and meandered towards the palace as lazily as the two streams bordering it wound through an ancient maze of forest monarchs. Clearly, palace gardeners kept the undergrowth down and the trees well pruned. Also, the place must have been protected by king's law, for gentle deer and bold rabbits watched me ride past without so much as a blink. No hunting allowed here.

Stalker tread the crushed shells underfoot without the slightest hint of agitation. The spot was so calm I did not wonder at Mercy having been raised here. Such a sweet-natured girl; no other surroundings would have suited her half so well.

I rounded a bend in the lane which took me out from under the canopy and into the midst of gardens more wondrous than I can describe. The hedges had been shaped into all manner of fantastic birds and beasts. Multiple rows of red roses perfumed the air, and other varieties of flowers were not absent. It was a manmade paradise, complete with fountains spurting crystal water, natural arbors, marble benches, and beautifully carved statues of knights and maidens, lords and ladies, and nymphs and dragons.

From the gardens, I had a perfect view of the palace itself. There was no protective wall. In an enchanted place like this, what need for military defense? The main portion was but three stories high at most, low and sprawling as castles go, yet stylish in its architecture. Built of beige stone, its many roofs and towers were topped with gleaming black tiles. The royal standard of Merris flew from each spire, while on the square towers could be seen a few guards standing lookout. Behind the castle itself, glimpses could be caught of a great pool of water, a square arch supported by fat columns, a tennis court, stables, and even a fine cow byre.

Apart from my Mercy, it was the most beautiful sight I had ever seen, and I pulled Stalker to a halt that I might admire it.

This is perfection, I thought, a little worry stealing in to mix with the awe. *Perhaps this is why Mercy said she would not wed me. Perhaps she's no wish to leave such a place.*

For the first time, the idea that my princess might not love me enough to want to leave father, mother, kindred and home invaded my mind, evoking a stab of fear.

I can build her a fine home, but I cannot compete with this.

Perhaps the beauty of her home was not the reason at all, though. Whatever it was, I had to find out. Nudging Stalker with my heels, we set off again.

At the palace gate I gave my name to the head guard; a needless thing to do since, judging from his gawking at my horse and the emblem on my shield, he'd already guessed my identity.

"Sir Buckhunter Dornley to see his royal majesty, King Merl of Merris," I announced formally. "Will you escort me to him, my good man?"

"A—at once, Sir Knight," the stubby, armored man replied, his whiskered chins quivering and his eyes wide. A bead of sweat trickled down his temple from beneath his conical helmet, which was topped with a brilliant blue plume. The color was singularly unbecoming, poor fellow. "If you will follow me, I shall inform his majesty of your arrival."

Being the most famous knight in the land—nay, on the continent, does have its advantages, I prided myself, my fears of not being good enough dissipating nearly as fast as they'd come.

I followed the guard down lengthy passageways lined with rich tapestries, and each person we passed, highborn or low, stopped and stared. I'd purposely worn my chainmail and, over it, my white tunic embroidered with four purple dragons, their necks intertwined. The emblem, my trademark, ensured instant recognition, as did my height and build. I was distinctly taller than every man present, and hoped Mercy would have marked this.

Finally, we reached the king's receiving chamber, where I was announced and shown in.

"Welcome, welcome, Sir Knight," his majesty, Merl of Merris, greeted me heartily. "Please, be seated. Make yourself comfortable. My home is yours, you know." He waved me to a grand chair a pace or two from his.

As your daughter will be, soon enough.

"Thank you, Your Majesty." I bowed politely before seating myself in the spot he'd offered.

"To what do we owe the honor of a visit from the greatest knight in all of Gindsland?" Making a steeple of his fingers, King Merl shot me a speculative glace over his manicured fingertips. "Needless to say, I'd no idea Sir Buckhunter Dornley traveled my domain, or I would have prepared a royal welcome."

"No need for that," I responded lightly, brushing aside all formal pleasantries, "although I have come on an important mission. I have come to ask for your daughter's hand in marriage."

Dead silence filled the room. At first, his majesty stared at me blankly. When what I was saying sunk in, his eyes narrowed to gleaming slits and he began tapping his steepled fingers together.

"*You* wish to marry *my* daughter?"

I nodded.

"But you've not met the girl," he protested, an objection born from bewilderment rather than denial. No one, not even a king, would have scorned me as a prospective son-in-law. "Not only that," he continued, "but I was under the impression that you were...ah, rather averse to the idea of taking a bride."

I merely smiled, willing to let him think what he chose. "Nonetheless, I have decided to marry, and your daughter is the maiden of my choice. I am willing, Your Majesty, to pay whatever bride price you set, as well as engage myself in your services for...a fixed number of years," I finished carefully.

Although I wanted Mercy and was prepared to give anything for her, there was no need to enslave myself to her manipulative father. And manipulative King Merl was; his reputation preceded him. As we discussed stipulations, why not try to get myself the better end of the bargain and Mercy to boot?

"Sir Buckhunter Dornley in my services?" Merl of Merris echoed, the light of greed springing to his eyes. "A boon indeed! What a march I would be stealing upon my enemies."

"Don't forget the bride price," I reminded him.

"You have, naturally, heard of my wealth."

"Naturally, naturally," the king agreed, those fingers tapping more briskly as each second passed. "Hmmm..."

For my part, I remained silent, watching the wheels in that grey head spinning. That he was also determined to get the better end of the deal was plain to see. Well, I was prepared to bend. As long as I walked away with Mercy on my arm, I'd be satisfied.

A minute or two passed while the king ruminated on the projected offer. Then, straightening abruptly in his throne-like chair, he signaled a nearby servant.

"Call my daughter and heir," he ordered. "Say that her father has marvelous tidings to share."

The servant scurried away to do as bidden, and King Merl turned to me. Shameless conniving was written all over his bearded face. "Now, Sir Knight, let us talk terms."

It may have been from her father that Mercy obtained her small stature, her blue eyes, and her brown-blonde hair (albeit his was somewhat darkened by grey), but her wholesome, guileless nature must have come entirely from her mother. King Merl haggled better than a seller in the marketplace. By the time a herald arrived to announce the princess's advent, I'd agreed to a steep bride price, and had also signed away ten years of my life in service to the kingdom of Merris. Hefty payments, yes, but I didn't care. Excitement built as I watched the doorway through which she'd come, longing to see her...

The princess came, but she was not at all the maiden I'd expected. This woman was a year or two older than Mercy: tall, slim, and coldly handsome. The black velvet of her figure-hugging gown emphasized her pale skin and frosty, wraithlike beauty. Whereas Mercy was a gust of springtime air, a burst of summer sunshine, a field of flowers beside a babbling brook, this woman was ivory moonlight on winter's snow. Icy, ashen, exquisite.

"You sent for me, Father?" she inquired formally, halting beside the man. Her ice-blue eyes fastened on me, and in them I saw the same speculative, gleaming glint as the king's.

"I did, Venda," he responded. "You see before you Sir Buckhunter Dornley, the most famous—and, may I say, the wealthiest?—knight in the empire. He has come seeking your hand in marriage."

Some terrible mistake had been made. I got to my feet, raising my hand in protest.

"Wait, no—that is not what I said at all!"

His majesty was perplexed. "Did you, or did you not, request the hand of my daughter in marriage? Well, this is she."

"No, Princess Venda is not who I meant," I blustered angrily, confused. "It is Mercy I would take to wife."

"*Mercy?*"

Lovely Princess Venda and her father gasped the name in unison.

"Yes, Mercy," I shot back. "She, too, is your daughter, is she not?"

Before the king or princess had a chance to reply, there came a soft call from the doorway in a voice I knew well.

"Buck?"

I whirled to see her standing there. Her eyes were

red from weeping, and her face was splotchy. Her hair was slipping from the loose knot confining it, and her clothing was untidy, but never in my life had I seen a vision more alluring.

"What are you doing here?"

She advanced a few steps into the room, and I noticed the wet handkerchief wadded in her hand.

"Mercy..."

I could not help myself. Hardly knowing what I did, unable to bear seeing her in tears, I turned my back on her father and sister and strode toward her, catching her hands, hankie and all, in mine.

"Mercy, love, do not cry. All will be well, you'll see." I smiled bravely, hoping to ease her fears. "I've come to ask your father for your hand in marriage. He has agreed; the terms are set. Mercy, my love, with your consent we will be married soon. I swear it."

Mercy's gasp of horror was matched only by her sister's shriek of terror. The next thing I knew, Princess Venda had crumpled to the floor in a dead faint. Breaking free of me, Mercy ran to her sister, while the king regarded both of his daughters with abject dismay.

"What did I say?" I wondered aloud, but it was to be quite some time before I'd obtain an answer.

After being assured by the stablemaster that both Stalker and my belongings would be well cared for, I was shown by the palace majordomo to a fine bedchamber to await a summoning by the king. I consumed the supper served in my room in miserable, brooding silence, speculating as to what witchery was going on. So I'd come seeking Mercy's hand in marriage: was that cause for everyone in Merris to gape at me as if I had three eyes in my face or six fingers on my hand?

Even the servants and majordomo had regarded me strangely. Clearly, everyone around here knew something I didn't. Something I was almost as determined to find out as I was to have Mercy to wife.

Later that evening—it must have been a little past eight of the clock, for the sun was near gone, leaving the sky a cobalt easel streaked with gold and flame—there was an unexpected knock on my door. Already I had washed, shaved, and changed into simple, comfortable clothing. A servant had come for the supper tray, and I was anticipating no guests. Still, when I heard that timid tapping, my heart leapt in my chest, for I hoped it might be the girl I was longing to see.

"Yes, who is it?" I called, rising to my feet.

Let it be Mercy. Please let it be Mercy.

"It is Lady Stazia del Vanderdyke," came the reply. "Please, Sir Dornley, may I enter? I've something to say to you."

Lady Stazia del Vanderdyke? Well did I remember her, the twit. Although, come to think of it, she could not be as great a twit as her sister, for Lady Stazia had been the one to insist I was alive, not dead. She was also, if memory served me correctly, the person who had first suggested asking the princess about my condition. Which meant I was in her debt. If she hadn't, would I have ever met my beloved?

For that reason, I bade her enter, and used my most courteous manners as I insisted she take the finest chair in the room, which happened to be the only chair in the room. Ah well. Since there was nowhere else to sit, I sank to the edge of the bed, clasping my hands as I waited for her to speak.

She was anxious and ill at ease. Her round cheeks were slightly flushed, and she perched on the very edge of the chair, as if prepared to spring up and dart away. Determined to give her no cause, I kept my movements small and my voice slow.

"Well, my lady, here you are. What did you wish to speak with me about?"

"Sir Dornley—"

"Please," I interrupted, determined for Mercy's sake to be as kind as possible, "call me Buck."

"Very well then, Sir Buck, I—forgive my intruding like this, but Rosy said she would not go and that I must go, as I was the braver of us. I said perhaps Princess Mercy should go, but you simply cannot expect a young woman to—"

"Lady Stazia, please! What is it you have come to say?"

I couldn't conceal my frustration. Was there any woman in Gindsland who was capable of coming to the point without running down rabbit trails and beating around every rose bush in the royal gardens first?

"What?" She seemed irked at being interrupted, but thankfully recalled her mission. "Oh yes, well, Sir Buck, what I have to say is this."

She drew herself upright in the chair, smoothing her skirts over her knees. Lifting her chin and meeting my gaze with surprising boldness, she said,

Knight's Rebirth

"Sir Buckhunter Dornley, though you be a knight most worthy, wealthy, and true, it is my painful duty to demand that you leave this palace and the kingdom of Merris. Tonight! No good can possibly come of your suit to win the princess's hand. It is best for all involved if you would simply forget Mercy, as I've no doubt she, herself has told you."

"Wait, wait!" This was the second time during my short stay in these lands that I'd been ordered to leave. I liked it no better coming from the lips of Mercy's attendant than I had coming from the Curator. "Did Mercy bid you say this to me? Did she put these words in your mouth?"

"What? How could you think such a dreadful thing of my dear friend?" The young lady was offended and snorted daintily to show her displeasure. "Mercy had nothing to do with this. It was her sister's idea—Princess Venda, you know."

"Princess Venda?" Now I was more puzzled than ever. "Why would Princess Venda not want me to marry her sister? Does she hate me that much? Or is it Mercy she hates?"

"Hates? She hates neither of you, but you cannot marry Mercy, and Venda will marry no one who lacks royal blood. Which means, as I have said, that it's best for all involved if you would simply..."

I didn't hear the rest. For an instant, when she'd started that little speech, which I was fairly certain the ice princess had fed her, I'd felt cold fear seize my limbs. Was this Mercy's way of denying my request? Did she return none of my tender feelings? However, now that I was aware the message had come from her sister, I felt tremendous relief. Not Mercy's idea, after all. Maybe there was still hope.

"Lady Stazia," I began carefully, knowing I likely tread on dangerous ground, "has Princess Mercy spoken to you...of me, I mean?"

"But of course!" the maiden replied. "She is my dear friend. We share all."

"And what does she—what does she think of me? Do you think she would favor my suit?"

"What does she think of you? Do I think she would favor your suit?" The girl's dark brows knit in a frown. "What silly questions. Don't you know?"

I swallowed hard, fearing my voice would crack. "Um...how would I know, my lady? Know for sure?"

"Brilliant stars above, you men really are dense, aren't you?" She gave her head a toss, suddenly wise and knowing beyond her years. "If you cannot interpret her behavior by now, I suppose you never will."

I sat there unable to speak, my hands clasped so tightly my knuckles had turned white. She decided to take pity on me. The meaningful look melted off her features. Her mouth sought to repress a teasing smile, a smile her eyes could not hide.

"I could tell you," she offered, "but that would spoil the fun, wouldn't it? No, I think you should ask Mercy yourself. If you are brave enough to slay dragons, win tournaments, and even ask his majesty for her hand, then you should be brave enough to do that, shouldn't you?"

"But—"

She had already risen to her feet. The smile blooming on her pretty face was bittersweet. "I take it I've failed in my mission. You will stay?"

She knew my answer before I gave it. "Wealth and fame could not tempt me to leave. Wild trolls could not drag me away."

"You have no idea what you've gotten yourself into," she replied, blinking rapidly to dispel tears. "But if you love her that much—"

"I do," I replied earnestly, rising as well. "Believe me, my lady, I do."

"So I suspected," she said softly, sounding closer and closer to crying. "So I told Princess Venda, but she insisted on one of us coming. Well, it is not my fault if I failed."

She left, and I slumped into the chair she'd vacated, my mind in turmoil. Why would Mercy's elder sister be so averse to my wedding her sibling? More importantly, what did Stazia know that I did not? Could Mercy's feelings be so transparent that I ought to know something I didn't? Did I have the courage to ask?

CHAPTER NINE
Of Threats, Balls, and Kisses

This was a strange family. A strange kingdom. A strange palace. I did not know what to think, who to believe, or what to expect.

King Merl I did not trust.

Princess Venda I trusted even less.

I could not form an opinion of Lady Stazia. Even though she had come to warn me away, she'd also seemed rather sympathetic to my plight. Still, I knew not to place too much faith in her.

And Mercy? Of course, I trusted Mercy implicitly. At this point, what I needed was to make her trust me. Not only that, I needed to hear her say she loved me. Those would be words worth living—and dying—for.

The next morning, shortly before the noon hour, with Lady Stazia's words and my questions ringing in my ears, I stood again before the ruler of Merris. Like his daughter's the previous day, his eyes were red, yet

I suspected it was a redness caused by lack of sleep rather than weeping. Neither Mercy nor her sister was present. I was given no opportunity to inquire as to their whereabouts, for with no ceremonial overtures a haggard King Merl opened his mouth and began to speak.

Mercy was his youngest child, he said, younger than twenty-one year old Venda by three years. In Merris, the younger is rarely given in marriage before the elder. Moreover, Mercy was also...well, to put it bluntly, the less attractive of the two, and not heir to the throne, like her sister. Was I certain I would not reconsider Venda's hand in marriage? He would half, or even relinquish, both the obligatory bride price and the years spent in service to himself.

I shook my head stubbornly, feeling a growing annoyance that the man deemed me so fickle. As if any honorable knight would change his choice of wife for either money or years of service. I had my faults, but fickleness was not one of them. Had money or military service meant anything to me, I would have been married long ago—and to a girl whose father was willing to pay me to take his daughter off his hands. No, it was love upon which I based my choice. I reaffirmed this to my intended's father.

"It is Mercy I love, and Mercy alone I will have," I stated firmly. "The terms we set are inconsequential. For your youngest daughter, I would gladly double both."

"I feared you would say that," he sighed. I was baffled by the misery in his tones.

Motioning me to a seat, he folded bejeweled hands in his lap.

"For Mercy, then, I ask neither a bride price nor

your services."

"Then what do you ask?" I returned, taken aback.

"For Mercy I demand a boon, a favor. A deed to prove your valor, one that will demonstrate to the world that you are truly worthy of my youngest daughter."

I fought to conceal my surprise. This was certainly a switch! His eldest daughter he'd all but guaranteed free of charge, as it were. For Mercy I must "prove my valor," which had been proven ten thousand times already, as he was fully aware. Nevertheless, I was not about to argue, not when there was a chance of obtaining my heart's desire.

"Tell me what I must do," I demanded, leaning towards him.

That night, a grand ball was held in my honor. His majesty had made me swear not to speak to anyone concerning our bargain. I found his behavior extraordinarily strange, and his bargain even stranger, but what could I do? I loved Mercy, and if wedding her meant risking my life first in the land of Dead Derion, then I had no alternative.

I tamed my dark, wavy hair with a comb and water before dressing in my finest coat, trousers, and tall boots, which I had polished to a glossy sheen. Standing beside his majesty, I listened to the same fashionable majordomo introduce me to the gathered crowd. The answering cheers seemed somewhat strained.

What was wrong with everyone in this palace? It just went to demonstrate, I suppose, that outward beauty did not mean a perfect interior.

Come to think of it, Princess Venda was much like her palace.

As the guest of honor, I was obligated to open the ball by dancing with the queen of Merris, Mercy's mother. She was as lovely as her daughters, both of them, with Venda's stature and Mercy's summery allure. Her manner was polite, if reserved, a combination of Mercy's warmth and Venda's detachment. All in all, I decided she was an astonishing combination of both daughters, or else both had inherited several obvious physical and personality traits from her.

Following our dance, the king led his queen to the center of the floor, while I danced with their eldest daughter. She was not my partner of choice. What I wanted more than anything was to be whisking Mercy around the chandelier-lit ballroom, rather than her conceited sister. But protocol must be kept, so I danced with Princess Venda, holding her as gingerly as one might hold a venomous reptile.

Speaking of reptiles, the hooded look she slanted me after a few moments of dancing was positively that. Reptilian. Somehow, it managed to turn my blood cold and raise my ire all at the same time.

Pity the fool who marries her, I decided, remembering her father's entreaties for me to do just that. Doubtless, what he really wanted was for someone to take her off his hands.

The first thing she said to me was, "I hear tell that Lady Stazia's visit was fruitless. She says that *wild ogres could not drag you away*. Really, Sir Knight, such boyish bravado does you little credit. You would be a great deal more impressive if you would show a man's wisdom by simply leaving my sister alone, as everyone wants you to do."

"Oh?" I asked, straining to keep from either erupting like a volcano or shaking loose from her chilly touch. "Is that your opinion, Your Highness, or the opinion of the entire realm?"

"If you mean my simpering sister," she snapped, casting a haughty glance towards Mercy, who watched with Stazia and Rosy from the borders of the room, "what she thinks is her own business. She is far too simpleminded to know what is best for her or Merris, and certainly too lenient to insist upon anything. I am warning you that you will regret it if you stay here. For your own welfare, as well as Mercy's and that of the entire kingdom, you would be wise to pack up and leave." Her eyes narrowed to slits, her scowl rivaling the ugliest glare from the meanest dragon I'd ever faced. "*Tonight.*"

The music had drawn to a close. The princess and I came to a standstill. I was more than happy to drop my hands and release her.

"Say what you like, Princess, but I am not about to leave. If I should die in her behalf, I would not regret it."

She smiled an evil smile, so frosty it froze the marrow in my bones. "Stay, and that may be your fate, fool."

After a mockingly low, elegant curtsey, she turned on her heel and glided away. I shivered, but it was a shiver that instantly dissolved when a small hand touched my back. A sweet voice said, "Buck?"

I spun, nearly giddy with relief when I saw the

sister of that tall, blonde viper.

"Mercy..." I didn't bother trying to hide my joy.

"Buck, are you well?" Her smile was wary, and worry darkened her eyes. "I saw you dancing with Venda, and neither of you looked very happy, and—"

A definite understatement.

"If there is anything I can do—"

"Yes," I agreed, "there is. You can dance with me."

"Oh dear." She hedged a step away. "I warned you earlier that I do not dance gracefully."

"Nonsense!" I protested, and swept her up into my arms.

The musicians struck up a waltz, and in an instant we were whirling about the floor. Boldly, I pulled her close, and to my joy she succumbed without protest. I don't know why she claimed to be a poor dancer; she was as fine a companion as a man could wish. I spent the next two sets enjoying her presence and working up my courage. Then the time had come, the time for me to act upon Lady Stazia's suggestion. It could not be put off any longer, no matter what Stazia, Merl, or Venda had advised.

"Mercy?"

"Yes, Buck?"

Was it my imagination, or had the worry in her face been replaced by...dreaminess?

"I...um...you...we..."

Curse me for the fool Venda considered me, but every rational thought fled with her so close. How was a man supposed to think, let alone make such a delicate inquiry, when what he wanted more than life itself was clasped in his arms?

"Yes, Buck?"

A coy smile played about her mouth, a mouth I

suddenly wanted desperately to kiss.

"I, um, your friend, the Lady Stazia—she visited my room last night."

"Oh, did she?"

Something about the way she said that, the way she arched a brow, made me hot. "No, that is not what I meant at all! I mean, she visited my room last night on a mission for your sister. She had a speech prepared, and she—"

"Don't tell me, let me guess." Mercy was far from surprised. "Venda coaxed Stazia into asking you to leave. She claimed that no good can come of your staying here, is that it?"

I nodded.

"Is that what Venda was saying to you when you danced?" she inquired, tensing in my arms.

Again I nodded, but quickly added, "Yes, but that is not what I wanted to talk to you about."

"Did you think I had something to do with it? Because I didn't. I know I acted very strange yesterday in the woods, but you must understand—my position is rather difficult. I cannot explain everything now, and I know it must seem bizarre to you, what with first Stazia's visit and then Venda's warning, but let me assure you that it has nothing to do with you. You personally, I mean."

Sometime during the midst of this lengthy and rather incomprehensible speech, I had come to a staggered halt on the dance floor, oblivious to the other couples still spinning about us in a sea of color. Now I faced her, thoroughly confused.

"What?"

"Did you hear nothing I said? Oh Buck, sometimes you can be so—so obtuse!" She started to pull away.

I refused to let her go. This place was hardly conducive to any sort of important conversation, let alone figuring out Mercy's convoluted explanation.

"Come with me," I said, grasping her by the hand and guiding her through the maze of dancers.

"Buck, where are we going?"

"Outside," I answered, and sped up, taking her out the open doorway, down the veranda steps, and into the palace gardens beyond. Mellow, golden light spilled from the great floor-to-ceiling windows of the ballroom, bathing her skin in warm shades of amber and making her hair gleam like honey. As soon as it was safe, I whirled and whisked her into my arms to do something I'd been longing to do for quite some time: bend and steal a very long—and, may I say, very enjoyable—kiss.

"Buck!" she gasped, when I finally found the willpower to drag my mouth away.

"What?" I slid my fingers into her upswept hair, heedless of all the hard work that must have gone into the waterfall arrangement of curls and ribbons. It was silk against my skin, entrancing. "Don't tell me you haven't wanted that as much as I."

"Of course I...haven't," she tried to say, but the glow in her eyes betrayed the lie.

I bent to kiss her again. Rather than shy away, she returned it, melting against me, clinging to my shoulders as if my strength was what saved her knees from buckling.

"Buck, you must stop," she whispered, her fingers clenched in my coat front and her face upturned to mine. "Someone might see."

"So let them see."

"But what will they think?"

"What will they think? They will think they see a man and woman in love, who have come outside to steal a few moments in the moonlight. What is wrong with that? Are you ashamed to be thought my lover? Am I unworthy of you?"

"Hardly," she blushed, lowering her eyes.

From somewhere deep within came the certainty that this was the perfect moment, the opening I had been seeking.

"Then, you do love me?"

I was rewarded with the tightening of her curled fingers and the slow nod of her head.

"Yes," she admitted in a very low voice. "I do. How could I help it? I've never met anyone like you, you brave, arrogant, charming fool, with your too-large nose, too-large muscles, and too-large aura of self-importance."

Brave, arrogant, charming fool? Overlarge nose, muscles, and aura of self-importance?

"Not exactly the reasons a man wishes to hear why his woman loves him, but I will take whatever I can get if you will reconsider my marriage proposal. Will you at least think about it?" I pleaded, my heart in my throat.

"Oh Buck, you don't know what you're asking," she replied fearfully, her troubled eyes whisking over my face.

Oh yes, yes I do, I thought grimly, remembering King Merl's outlandish demands for his daughter's hand. But I had promised not to speak of them to anyone, especially her. Furthermore, I'd sworn to Venda that, should I die in her sister's behalf, it would not deter me. Considering the terms her father had set, that might not be an empty promise.

CHAPTER TEN
Of Boatmen and Cyclopes

The hour had come. It was time for me to put my money where my mouth was, so to speak. I had sworn that I would defend Mercy, even to the death, and this was the first test of those vows. I was no coward, nor was I a fool. (Or, if I was a fool, I wasn't a complete fool.) Something odd, something dreadful underlay King Merl's outrageous demands for Mercy, as well as Mercy's professing to love me but reluctance to marry me.

What was it?

Unfortunately, I would have to fulfill this quest and come back alive before I would find out.

I was tightening a strap on Stalker's saddle when she came to me. At the sound of my name I turned, smiling down at the woman I loved.

"Mercy," I said, forgoing my task and opening my arms instead. "Have you a kiss for the knight you love?"

To my astonishment, she flew into my embrace, only to cast her own arms about my waist, clutching me in a tight, desperate sort of grip.

"Buck," she whispered, face buried in my chest. "Don't do this, I pray. Whatever it is, wherever Father is sending you, don't go. I am not worthy. Please, please say you'll not go."

"Why, Mercy," I chuckled, easing her away and tilting her chin to see into her face. "What's this? Tears?" Gently, I wiped them away. "Do you fear to see me leave?"

Biting her lower lip, she shook her head. "No," she denied, "I fear never seeing you again."

"Tsk, tsk," I scolded playfully, trying to reassure her. "Such little faith you have in me. Am I not a very famous knight? You know my reputation. How can you doubt me?"

"I don't doubt you, Buck—I fear for you! How can you be so irritating?"

"Irritating?" Wrapping my arms around her, I drew her closer, smoothing a hand over her hair. "Say not irritating, my love. Say bold or daring or courageous, but do not say irritating."

"Buck—"

"No more objections, Princess," I interrupted, seeing her father step out onto the palace steps, probably to guarantee I didn't leak the news in the final moments before I left. "It is time for me to depart. Kiss me goodbye, and think of me often. Until I return, your prayers will be my shield and your love my defense."

Clearly, she wanted to argue, to do anything except comply. Nevertheless, in the end, she bravely choked back arguments and tears, straining up on tiptoe to twine her arms around my neck and pull me down for a kiss. Ignoring her father's presence, I returned the gesture, kissing her until she was breathless as I, then, reluctantly, let her go.

"Think of me," I urged once mounted, Stalker's reins captured firmly in my fist.

She nodded sadly, throwing me a final kiss as I put heels to my horse's flanks and galloped out the open palace gates.

Two days of hard riding brought me to the river Stixe, over which I must cross. Stixe was famous for the grey cloud of depression overhanging its waters, a cloud said to dishearten the hardiest of travelers.

Not me.

The evening may have been gloomy and foggy, but my spirits were abnormally high. Three tasks the king had set before me. Accomplish these, and Mercy would be mine.

On the brink of the river was a great, dead tree that must have been magnificent once. Now, its black limbs were broken and bare, and its crusty bark mostly stripped away by wind and weather. A raven perched on its branches, a raven with glittering, violet eyes, who cocked its head at me, blinked, and then flew away with an irritated caw as I approached. From one of the lower branches, a golden trumpet dangled from a leather cord. I seized it, put the instrument to my lips and blew a single, clear blast. From popular folklore, I knew this was the traditional summons for the ancient boatman whose craft ploughed these waters. After replacing the horn, I urged Stalker away from the tree and toward the shore.

"Now, we wait," I said to him, comforting the animal with a brisk rub of his muscular neck. Stalker did not like this place, and I could hardly blame him. Legend alleged the river was deep and wide, full of sucking whirlpools and treacherous currents. All but the wiliest sailors feared to sail it, and regular travelers were fools who chose some other means of crossing than what I planned to use.

Around us was a forest of dead trees, rotted with age and blasted from fire and wind. The raven was gone, and no living things beside the two of us were to be seen, except a pair of very hungry, very ugly vultures, brooding in a nearby tree. An ill omen? I suppressed a shiver and turned my back on the dismal scene.

What lay beyond the mists of Stixe was something of a mystery. Most folk dared not journey too far inland, but there was much speculation. Some believed it a place of dark magic and devious wizards, an area of either ill-gotten wealth or endless toil and pain. Others swore this mysterious land held the key to finding the desire of one's heart, be it good or bad, provided they possessed the courage to seek it. A few insisted the land held untold riches: that there was an ancient pirate treasure buried deep within the interior, guarded by a fierce band of cutthroat spirits. Others believed the secret to life eternal lay somewhere in the perfect middle of Dead Derion, the realm the river bordered.

The truth or falsehood of these beliefs, I did not

know. King Merl must have at least acknowledged some of the tales, for it was to Dead Derion that I had been sent.

An hour passed, then two. A dense, dank fog rolled over the river, headed towards the shore. Stalker shied nervously, holding his ground only because of my grip on the reins. I did not like that fog at all, and was prepared to retreat until I saw, borne upon the wings of water and fog, a long, sleek craft. In it was the ferryman, a bowed, wizened old man clad in a long scarlet robe. With a gentle bump, the prow touched land and came to rest. Swallowing my reluctance, I nudged Stalker forward.

"Payment," wheezed the ancient creature, extending a skeletal hand.

Withdrawing three silver coins from my purse, I dumped them into his palm. He examined them closely for a long, tense moment.

Finally, "This will do," he intoned, lifting cold, sunken eyes of blue. With a flick of his wrist, he beckoned us aboard.

Stalker disliked both the ferryman and his craft, yet we had no choice but to step inside. Maneuvering a large warhorse into a low-walled craft is no easy task. Fortunately, my mount trusted me implicitly. I didn't take my hand off his muzzle nor cease mumbling comforting little phrases as we sailed that dark river.

In the pale fog that rapidly enveloped us I saw writhing, twisting shapes of people, animals, and monsters in torment, but refused to show fear. The ferryman paid no more heed to them than he did to Stalker and me, but held his silence the entire crossing. No inquiries about who we were or where we were going. He did not care. He had his payment; that was all that mattered.

I was never so glad to depart a place as I was to leave that vessel and its eerie captain. After scouting out a somewhat sheltered spot in crumbling, ancient ruins that lay close by, we camped that night on the banks of the river. At least I had a wall to guard my back. Even so, I slept little, dozing while keeping an eye on my fire. The best deterrent to any unwholesome visitors, spirit or flesh, is a roaring fire, and I made sure mine blazed throughout the night. Thankfully, the hours passed quietly, and come the dawn, we were well on our way to finding the fabled Tree of Renewal, upon which apples of gold were said to hang.

The Tree was easily found, for the smoke of a nearby bonfire signaled the way for miles. Why I chose to follow this strange cloud, I cannot say. Possibly it was out of sheer curiosity. Also, I knew I must start looking somewhere, since I had no idea where the Tree was located. Smoke meant a fire, and fire meant someone had to have built it. Maybe that someone could give me information about my quest. That in mind, I pointed my destrier's nose in the direction of the smoke, and off we went.

Three hours before noon I came upon it, and was disgusted to discover it was an eternally burning bonfire, fed by a tremendous heap of human flesh and bone. The Tree itself, imposing and regal, stood approximately twenty paces away from the bonfire. Tearing my gaze from the horrid kindling, I saw to my surprise that it did indeed bear the remarkable fruit which King Merl sought.

"Lovely, isn't it?" croaked a voice from behind. I

whirled, pulling Stalker's head around, to face the guardian of the Tree.

A towering cyclops, he stood twice as tall as any man, including myself, and more than twice as broad. His copper-colored face was twisted and mashed, and looked as if it had been struck repeatedly by a gigantic fist. Sharp, white fangs poked out from the corners of his upper lip, and his hair was like a pile of blonde straw.

"What are you doing here, little man?" He crept towards me ominously, an ugly smile on his ugly face. "It is death even to desire fruit from my Tree, which means you've no business here, save as my next meal."

"I am come to kill you and take fruit from your Tree," I returned unflinchingly. He did not know I had faced dragons before. What was a cyclops in comparison to a dragon?

My cool words, my lack of fear, startled him. The one huge eye in the center of his forehead blinked rapidly.

"What? Bold words from such a tiny foe! Why, if I were to swallow you whole, you'd scarcely make a lump in my throat."

"Tiny I may be, monster, but I am more than man enough to slay you," I fired back, and put heels to Stalker's sides.

Having faced both dragons and men many a time, my horse responded gallantly to this new challenge. We dashed forward, charging the giant. Only at the absolute last second did I weave sharply to the right, evading the huge paw he swept my way. As I galloped past his leg, I slashed it with the tip of my sword, grinning like a madman at his howl of pain. Then I whipped my horse about and galloped by on the other side, doing the same to his left leg. Black blood spurted like a fountain.

The cyclops went insane, roaring curses as he wove on bleeding legs and flailed trunk-like arms to keep his balance. He lost the fight when I drove Stalker straight at him, impaling his knee with my weapon and burying the blade up to the hilt. His guttural cries soaked the air as he fell with a crash that shook the earth. As he dropped, he managed to wrench out the sword and cast it my direction. I ducked as my own blade whizzed over my head, actually dinging off my helmet, but I was far from deterred.

Leaping from Stalker's back, I jumped onto the monster's torso, hit his chest running and raced from his stomach up to his neck. One thrashing paw found me, knocking me onto my side. I swore in frustration but rolled as I fell, drawing my dagger. The cyclops continued to thrash and I was losing my purchase, sliding off him. I managed to snatch a wrinkle in his thick neck with one hand. Hanging there by one arm, I used my other hand to drive my dagger's long, serrated blade deep in the brute's throat, even as my feet scrabbled for purchase on his leathery skin. His gargling cry was choked with blood.

Perhaps some will not understand why I plunged that blade again and again into his thick, muscled neck, but I'm sure they would sympathize if images of the cyclops' terrible bonfire were as fresh in their minds as they were in mine. When he finally died, I let go of that neck fold and slid to the ground. Walking away from his mountainous corpse, I retrieved my sword. Climbing back up onto the brute,

Knight's Rebirth

I sunk the blade deep in that repulsive, single eye, cut it out, and tossed it upon its owner's bonfire, since the monster itself was too heavy to drag over.

There. Vengeance!

After plucking a golden apple from the Tree of Renewal and stowing it in my saddlebags—cushioned from potential bruises by all those favors of silk and satin—I left that scene of death and headed for another.

CHAPTER ELEVEN
Of Helpful Secrets and Mysterious Guardians

One down, two to go. Since the first Tree had been guarded by a cyclops, I figured there was a good chance the others would be too. This did not bother me overmuch. If I could kill one, I could kill another.

What I was not counting upon you will soon discover. As sometimes happens, this unexpected turn of events happened to be one of the most important things ever to befall me.

For several hours, Stalker and I rode in companionable silence. Shortly after leaving the cyclops' eye burning on his own bonfire, we entered a great forest, the likes of which I'd never seen. You may not believe me when I tell you this, but I swear some of those trees talked and moved. I had been raised that it was impolite to ignore anybody, but when every other tree for a mile keeps shouting, "Trespasser, trespasser," at you, you tire quickly of trying to reason with them. It didn't take me long to give up and retreat into a cocoon of indifference. Being rooted to the ground, they could not reach me anyway, so long as I stayed on the road.

Eventually, we passed that part of the forest and entered another. A large lake could be glimpsed through the trees. Its waters were as black as the ancient cypresses lining its grey, sandy shore. I wouldn't have been surprised to learn that beneath its dark surface lurked all manner of foul creatures such as snakes, water dragons, alligators, and preying fish with teeth. I was happy to ignore this lake—until I began to catch glimpses of ghosts watching me from behind the trees. They were wavy and insubstantial, but were most definitely dressed like pirates.

Could it be? If I turned aside and searched here, questioned or followed those ghosts, would they lead me to the fabled pirate treasure? I'll admit I was tempted by the notion of bringing Mercy a great chest brimming with pirate plunder. Nevertheless, in the end I decided against it. Time was of the essence, and I could not afford to waste any in searching for treasure when I had plenty of my own. Not to mention, Mercy was not the sort of person to be overly impressed with wealth and treasure, anyway.

I wasn't far past the lake when I realized that, although the ghosts had peered out at me with unfriendly stares, none of them had assaulted me. As with the talking trees, it was like the power of the road protected its travelers. That, or maybe the power behind the road. Whatever power it was, and wherever it came from, something was definitely keeping both my horse and me safe.

What?

My question was answered that very evening when Stalker and I came upon a wee glade in the middle of the woods. In its midst was a humble, pleasant cottage. Wispy ribbons of grey smoke curled from the stone chimney. The door was bright green, except for the painted leaves and vines crawling in gold across its surface. The matching shutters were open to the evening air. The whole place bore a restful, welcoming atmosphere.

"What have we here?" I murmured to my warhorse, who seemed as entranced by the woodsy cove as myself. "Shall we go and see?" He tossed his head up and down, giving assent. Chuckling, I slapped him affectionately on the neck. "Good boy. You always know the proper thing to say."

After tying Stalker to a large tree whose thick branches overhung the roof, I knocked on the cottage door.

"Who is there?" answered a frail voice.

"A traveling knight, Sir Buckhunter Dornley."

A pause. Then, "I've heard of you. Enter and be welcome, Sir Knight."

My fame had reached even this secluded spot? I must be more popular than even I'd realized.

Inside the cottage, the air was pleasant with the evening breeze and the scents of candles, a small fire, and the outdoors. In front of the river rock hearth sat an old woman with lively black eyes and quick, clever hands. Her once jet black hair was streaked with grey, but those nimble fingers never faltered as they worked the spinning wheel before her.

"Enter, enter," she called, nodding towards the

rustic chair across from her. "Be seated. Tell me what brings you to Dead Derion and the cottage of Pelinda the Guardian."

"Pelinda the Guardian?" I echoed, easing myself carefully into her chair. It was a bit small, and I half-feared it would collapse under my manly weight. "Pray, of what are you guardian?"

"Why of many things, son, including this road and all who travel it," she replied, as if I were ignorant for not knowing. Something about this reminded me of Mercy. "You've never heard of me?"

"No, but you seem to have heard of me," I replied, a bit testily. "Which is a curious thing, given the remoteness of your location."

"My road."

"I beg your pardon?"

"My road," she explained, "the road of which I am Guardian. There is not a single traveler who steps foot upon it, but my road communicates to me who they are and what is their purpose." Her hands never slowed, even when her beady black eyes lifted and fixed on my face. "Your objective is a difficult one. Did you not see the bonfire beside the Tree of Renewal? Flesh, my man, flesh. The burning bodies of all who have ever attempted to bypass the Guardian of the Tree and take its fruit."

"So the cyclops told me, yet you see what now smolders upon it."

"Indeed. You've a fine sense of justice."

Silence, save for the spinning, whirring, and clacking of her wooden wheel. "And now you think to slay his brothers and take fruit from their Trees, do you not?"

"I do."

"For what purpose?"

"Why not ask your road?" I taunted, spitefully pleased that it hadn't been able to disclose all of my secrets.

For that bit of insolence, I received a flashing glare and a sharp reprimand. "Do not mock me, young man!" the old crone snapped. "I've lived far longer than you, and have seen many proud, strutting peacocks like yourself come and go. If you wish me to help you in any way you must tell me your secrets."

"Why would I wish your help?" I asked, honestly puzzled. "Even if I did, why should I tell you my secrets? What could you possibly know that would be helpful to me?"

A sly smile curved the corners of her mouth, replacing the ire of a moment past. "Ah, a fair question. You do recall me saying that I was the Guardian of many things, including this road?"

"I do."

"Well, another matter over which I am Guardian is the future secrets that will aid those who travel my road."

"You mean—you can predict the future for me? Tell me what's going to happen and what I should do?" I leaned forward eagerly, hands on my knees, prepared to beg if that's what it took. For answers such as these, what wouldn't I give!

"Not exactly." She shook her head. "I cannot see into your future, nor can I predict the exact course your future will take. My wheel has told me, however, one particular secret that will be invaluable to you in days to come."

"Your wheel?"

I threw it a dubious glance. It looked like an

ordinary spinning wheel to me.

"Yes, my wheel. Do you, Sir Knight, wish to hear the secret of the wheel?"

"That depends," I hedged. "Do you mean the secret of how the wheel tells you these things, or the secret the wheel has told you that I will soon require?"

"Oh, the latter of course. You do not need to know the first."

"Very well, then. If you are willing to share it, I am more than happy to listen. I do have one question, however. Why are you willing to help me with this?"

She frowned, reproaching me. "Are you looking a gift horse in the mouth, Sir Knight?"

"Not at all. However, I have heard the tales. I know no one who works with magic offers their help without expecting something in return."

Her beady eyes narrowed to slits. At first, I thought she was angry, then the corner of her mouth lifted in a smile and she chuckled.

"You are wiser than your appearance would suggest," said she.

I was uncertain what to make of that remark.

"Yes, yes it is true that we who hold power like to get tit for tat. However, in this case, you have already done your part by helping my sister."

"I have?" I was genuinely perplexed. "Who is your sister?"

Pelinda waved a wrinkled hand. "You do not know her. However, you stole a march upon an old rival of hers whom she greatly detests. The Curator."

In my brain, a candle flickered to life. "The Curator. I remember him well."

"Rather difficult to forget, isn't he? He and that wolf of his." She turned her head and spat into the fireplace, causing the flames to sizzle. "He and my sister have been rivals for decades, there in Merl's lands. Until you came along and slayed his wolf. My sister reports he is a broken man, at least for now, and harasses her no further. So, because you have done my sister a good turn, I will do you a good turn and tell you the secret that you'll need in the future. After you tell me your purpose in seeking the enchanted fruit, of course."

Strange. When I'd met the Curator, I never expected the old grump to help me out in any way, but it seemed I was wrong. After telling my story, I listened without doubts or disbelief as Pelinda shared with me...well, really a most remarkable fact. I could not see how this secret, valuable though it was, would be of any immediate aid, but I hugged it close anyway, a talisman against the future.

The Guardian of the road insisted upon extending hospitality to Stalker and me. We accepted and spent the night under her protection, me in her cottage and Stalker safe in her glade. Both of us faced the next morning well fed and rested. Shortly after dawn, we were on our way to excitement, adventure, and the two other Trees. Not only had Pelinda shared with me the Secret of the Wheel, she'd also given instructions on how to reach the two remaining cyclopes. For this bit of information, she'd demanded payment. She wanted twigs from all three Trees, so she could plant more in her clearing. The Trees would be safe there, for she would become their Guardian along with all her other charges.

I did not mind this exchange. Fortunately, the golden apple from the Tree of Renewal had been plucked with a twig and leaves still attached. I broke them off and gave them to Pelinda. She accepted, but reminded me I still owed her twigs from the other Trees. I promised to deliver.

The old woman's directions were explicit. I reached the Tree of Rejuvenation before lunchtime, and the Livesaving Tree before dinner. I see no need to recount my battles with the cyclops' two elder brothers. Suffice it to say, both were as ugly and mean as their sibling. Both of them also had enormous, eternal bonfires fed by human remains. Even though both threatened to cast my body into the flames, in the end it was their repulsive, single eye—just like their brother's—that fed their infernos.

My reputation as a skilled fighter was not mere exaggeration.

Backtracking to Pelinda's hut, I presented her with the promised shoots. In return, she let me pass another night in her sheltered grove, and the next morning showed me a shortcut through the trees that led me swiftly to the banks of the river Stixe. This shortcut was not protected by her magic, and she warned me that I might have to do some fighting before I reached the river.

She was right. One bend in the path saw me assailed by a pack of grinning, rattling skeletons waving swords. Their movements were jerky and choppy, and I was able to fend them off fairly easily at first. It would not have been too difficult of a fight had not their numbers kept increasing as they popped up out of holes in the ground like moles from their hills. The only way to permanently dismantle them was to sever skull from spine. Once I figured this out, I was better able to protect myself. Even Stalker joined the action, using his hind legs to knock a skull or two from its neck.

We disentangled ourselves from that group with but a few nicks and scratches between us. A more difficult fight was the pair of harpies, whose forest nest we unwittingly passed under. My only warning was a screech from above, and then one of the grinning, gruesome creatures dropped from a lofty branch, right onto my back. Stalker whinnied and shied, which knocked me to the side, but also preserved him from the other harpy who had dove at him. Their faces and hair were like beautiful women, which made the rest of their appearance with grey, gristly skin and eagle wings and claws even more distorted.

The two beasts dragged me off my horse with their great talons, but by writhing and twisting madly I managed to get a deep slice on the talons of one with my dagger. She dropped me with an angry screech, leaving my entire weight for her twin to bear. The monster couldn't handle it; I was wearing full armor, after all. Even as she dropped me I reached up to grab her around her bird ankle, above her talons. I pulled her down with me as I landed on my back, and put my dagger to work, stabbing up into her belly. She screamed and howled like a human woman, while her twin dove at me, screeching. I had to release the one and spin to avoid my face being sliced to ribbons by the other, but by this point they'd had enough. Once I let go, they darted off and flew away wounded, one bleeding from her talons and the other her torso.

That was not the end of our adventures, but I spare you. Eventually, weary from warfare, both of us covered with dust and dried blood, only a few days after arriving in Dead Derion, Stalker and I crossed the river on the boatman's craft and retraced our steps toward the Kingdom of Merris. Now, along with the golden apple from the Tree of Renewal, a silver apple from the Tree of Rejuvenation and a ruby apple crowned with emerald leaves from the Livesaving Tree were safely stashed in my saddlebags.

His majesty cannot deny me now, I thought proudly as Stalker clip-clopped along. *I've more than proved my worth. He can have nothing else to say. What other knight could have braved the ferryman twice, killed those three monsters, and taken the plunder from their Trees?*

No one but Sir Buckhunter Dornley, of that I was convinced. I was also convinced that, when King Merl saw me returning in triumph with the spoils he'd sent me to fetch, he would be forced to agree, forced to uphold his end of the bargain. Provided she consented, Mercy would be mine. Nobody, or nothing, would stand in our way.

CHAPTER TWELVE
Of Apples and Graves

Now that I had completed the king's foolish, yet dangerous quest, I was determined to know the reason behind it. When he finally told me, I began to catch a glimmering of how Pelinda's secret might be necessary in the future, but for all my guesses, nothing could have prepared me for the ugly reality I was about to face. A reality that included murder.

My murder.

My murder at Mercy's hand.

It is this part of the story I'm the most reluctant to share, for I fear you will not understand why she did what she did. I can only beg you, as you read the following pages, to search your heart with extreme honesty. If you somehow found yourself in her predicament, her terrible, terrible predicament, what would you have done? It's a question nobody can answer for you. We would all have to answer it for ourselves. As Mercy did for herself.

When I presented the three magical apples to his majesty, he accepted them with wide eyes and trembling fingers.

"You—you did it," he stammered. "You killed the three cyclopes. You took the fruit. You returned alive and unharmed."

He gaped up at me, and this time the glint in his eyes had nothing to do with greed. I couldn't shake the feeling that it was fear. But of what was he afraid? I'd completed his three tasks. He owed me some sort of explanation as to the mysteries swirling about his family, his palace. I was not about to let him off the hook. So, seating myself without being invited, I blurted out a simple, five word question.

"What is going on here?"

King Merl glanced up sharply. "I'm sure I don't know what you are talking about."

"And I am sure you do," I returned coldly. "Do not presume me a fool, Your Majesty. I have eyes, and I can see that all is not right within your realm."

I went on to recount a few observations I'd made, including the sisters' strange behavior when I'd asked for Mercy's hand; the practically paying me to take Venda, while for Mercy I must risk life and limb; the palace servants' odd stares; Venda sending Stazia to talk me into leaving; the king's own nervousness. In summation, I added, "I am not a man easily deceived. Pray, tell me what goes on."

Wearily, King Merl of Merris laid aside the fruit,

placing it on an elegant red cushion decorated with gold tassels and braid. Defeat was on his face, in his voice. With a tired sigh he closed his eyes, slumping in his chair like a much older man.

"You are too clever by half, Sir Knight. I fear the truth can be concealed no longer."

"Tell me, then," I urged, leaning forward eagerly.

Later, I sought out the woman I loved, discovering her in the royal gardens, seated beside the same rosebush bursting with large, red blossoms where I had first kissed her. A few bees buzzed about, diving into the heart of a rose and out again, but my beloved took no notice. Instead, her gaze was riveted upon a nearby statue of a charging knight on his noble steed. It gleamed in the afternoon sunlight, its white marble free of lichen and moss. From the strength of her stare, it seemed to mean something special to her, and I flattered myself that was because of me.

And perhaps our first kiss. That was a memory I would certainly never forget.

"Mercy?" I announced my presence by calling her name.

"Buck!"

At the sound of my voice, her head whipped about. Relief sprang to her eyes. She leapt to her feet and ran to me. I opened my arms to receive her, crushing her close, holding her like the treasure she was. Oh, it felt good to hold her, even better now than before, now that I was aware of the deadly forces surrounding her. I couldn't resist bending for another kiss, wondering as I did at her steadfast good humor and courage.

"Oh Buck, you've come back to me," she murmured when my mouth had lifted from hers. She reached up to trace my face with her hand. "I was so afraid you would not."

"I will always come back to you," I vowed, running my calloused palm lightly over her silk-soft hair. "I love you so..."

"Buck..." She stepped back a little. "The night of the ball, Venda told me what was happening: that Father was sending you on some foolish quest. Both Venda and Father refused to tell me where until after you'd gone so I could not prevent you going. I am so sorry. It was unfair of him to send you on that mission. He thought you would—"

"Die? I know. I know that was his plan. Anyway, it would have made no difference if you had been privy to my destination and tried to dissuade me. I still would have gone. Besides, the only blame in this mess lies squarely upon the king. He confessed, Mercy. He told me everything."

"You know?" Her lovely blue eyes widened.

"I know," I muttered grimly, pulling her a little closer, holding her a little tighter. "I know, and I swear to you that you will not be offered in sacrifice to a dragon. No, nor your sister, either," I added, seeing the objections that leaped to her eyes.

"But, Buck, what can you do?" she cried, clutching two fistfuls of my tunic. "This is not any mere dragon: it's Triplehorn Wingback, the only creature, man or beast, ever to best you!"

"Best me?" I sputtered, somewhat indignantly. "Triplehorn never bested me. Twice, we fought to a draw."

"Bested or beaten, what does it matter?"

Frustrated, she turned and would have pulled away, but I caught her and tugged her backwards into my chest. Wrapping her up so tightly she couldn't move, I laid my unshaven cheek on top of her head. Upon my arrival at the palace, I had gone straightway to King Merl, determined to have the truth and uncaring about my appearance. Perhaps I should have cleaned away the dust and grime from travel before seeking Mercy out, not to mention shave, but clearly she did not care, so I let the thought slide.

"Mercy, Mercy, let us not quarrel," I pleaded. "There is a way, and we will find it. Have faith, sweetheart. Ancient customs cannot conquer our love."

At first she was stiff, noncompliant, but when I called her my sweetheart the rigidness left her body. She melted against me. Hearing her sniff, I knew tears had begun to flow. With all my heart, I wished that I might steal away her pain.

Now I understood why, back in my campsite in her father's woods, the day we played Questions she had told me, *If we are only to be friends for a short time, at least we are friends for now.* She lived with a sword of doom hanging over her head. She truly hadn't known how long she would be able to be my friend, and my potential leaving had nothing to do with that.

"You cannot know how hard it is to keep faith with death staring you in the face each and every day," she whispered. A wet drop spattered on my hand as I rocked her gently back and forth. "I try to be brave, but in the end, brave or coward, it will not matter. I am the second child. I am not heir to my father's throne. Instead, I have grown up knowing I am destined to give my life for this kingdom. I had a choice: I could be bitter at fate, or I could live in such a way that, when the time comes, I could look back and believe that both my life and my death have counted for something."

"Your life has counted for something," I encouraged her, running my hands caressingly over her upper arms. "Remember how you said you always try to bring happiness to others? What life is nobler than that? It is what you do and what you've always done. Nothing counts more than a life so lived."

She sniffled loudly. "Truly?"

"Mercy..." Gently, I grasped her by the shoulders, turning her about to face me. "You and you alone changed me from a hardened, selfish man destined to live a lonely life and die a lonely death, to a caring man whose strength is found in someone else. A man who loves and would do anything to enjoy that love. You, Mercy. Does that not count for something?"

She smiled sadly. "You were never hardened and selfish. You had a good heart all along; you simply needed someone to help you recognize it."

When I started to protest, she stopped me by laying her fingertips over my mouth. "No, I will not hear it. You are not perfect, none of us are, but you are the first and only person who ever..." She drew a deep breath, her shoulders rising and falling. "...who ever thought I was worth fighting, and possibly dying, for. You cannot know what that means to someone like me, someone who has lived their entire life under the shadow of self-sacrifice for the greater good.

"The last princess who died—she was my aunt, my father's sister. Did you know I was named for her? All my life, I was told how bravely she went to her fate. She didn't shed a single tear. She was held up as the highest example of honor and courage. I think of her and I think of the other princesses who lost their lives to a dragon. Were they afraid? I'm so afraid, Buck, but what is my life in comparison to my kingdom?"

Her words tore savagely at something inside of me. Anger flared. Anger at her father, a king, for choosing the coward's way out and simply acquiescing to an ancient curse instead of using all the means at his disposal to fight it. He had seen his sister perish and now would watch his daughter do the same without lifting a finger to prevent it. The worst cowardice here was his. My anger extended to her family, her mother and sister, as well as her kingdom for willingly watch her grow up like a lamb to the slaughter, uncaring for her fate as long as they were safe.

"Your aunt was greatly wronged," I told her. "But she did not have me to fight for her. You do. There is no person and no cause more worthy of fighting or dying for. I would hazard my life a thousand times over if it meant ensuring your safety for one more day."

"Oh Buck, I'm frightened," she confessed, collapsing and clinging to me like a vine clings to a tree for support. "Every day it becomes harder to face life with a smile. Now, in the end, fate sends me someone to love, and I fear I'll never get the chance to enjoy that love."

"You will," I promised her. "We'll find a way around this. You will be my wife, for I'll have no other. Nothing can come between us. Not even a dragon and an ancient curse. I vow it."

A solitary tear trickled from beneath her closed, wet lashes. I couldn't decide whether she believed me or not.

"Kiss me, Buck," she finally whispered. "Just kiss me."

I wanted to say more, to make her believe my words were true. However, I sensed mere words were not what she needed at this time. So I lowered my mouth to hers and kissed her with all the love that was inside of me, attempting to reassure her with my touch and my passion that everything would be all right.

That was the last time we were happily together. The very next morning, following an exquisite breakfast, Mercy invited me to accompany her on a stroll through the palace gardens. Like all men in love, I was oblivious to anything except the chance of getting my lady alone. I was so eager to enjoy her company that I paid no heed to her sad, weary eyes, or the way she kept touching the oddly shaped pouch at her waist.

When we reached the same bush of red roses, I made free to pull her into my arms. When I kissed her, I found myself a bit surprised by how passionately she responded. Even though she'd never been shy or timid, her kisses that day went to a bolder depth than, outside of marriage, I thought she would go. Enchanted by the magic she wove, I was caught completely off-guard when she slipped that dagger out of its pouch and between my ribs.

I now know those audacious kisses were her way of saying goodbye. Likewise, I suspect the redness of her wet eyes was the mark of a woman having spent the previous night in the deepest torment of soul. What a choice: deciding between the life of your sister and the man you wish to marry. Between a future with him, and a future that promises your own death by a dragon. Had you or I been in her place, what would we have done? How can anyone possibly judge her unless they have faced something similar?

Compounding matters, I've no doubt her father and sister put all sorts of pressure on her. Her father's scheme to kill me off by sending me on a wild quest in Dead Derion had failed, so they had to convince her another way. I'm sure I shall never know the anguish my poor, sweet Mercy endured that night while I slept peacefully in my bed, dreaming of the time she'd be forever at my side. For that, I blame myself. Had I used better judgment, really considered what I knew about King Merl and his conniving eldest daughter, I'd never have left Mercy's side. But what will be will be and what happened, happened.

As related at the beginning of this narrative, I died with my beloved's pleas for forgiveness ringing in my ears. I awoke, after a fashion, and rose invisible from my grave, only to find her weeping still.

"Oh Buck, it didn't work," she sobbed, her fingers buried in the loose dirt covering my buried body. "I was so positive it would, or I would never have taken this chance. How can you forgive me? What have I done? I've murdered the man I love!"

She did not see me, for I was in spirit form, like a ghost. I hovered overhead, listening to her puzzling words. Strangely, I felt no anger toward her. A bit of resentment, perhaps, that she hadn't had enough faith in me to believe I would find a way out of our predicament, but I loved her too much and understood too well why she'd done what she'd done to be angry with her. Not to mention, I was completely mystified by what she was saying.

What had failed to work? Of what had she been so positive? And, yes, she certainly had killed the man she loved—how could she not have known it until now, possibly hours later? Long enough for my body to be taken and buried. What did she think happened when you stabbed someone repeatedly with a knife?

Perplexed, but desperate to comfort her, I floated along as she tread sorrowfully from my grave in the forest (apparently, I'd been given a secret, hasty burial, so the entire incident of my courting Mercy might be forgotten) to her own bedchamber in the palace. There, she collapsed upon her bed and wept for a long time. Anxious, I whisked back and forth, cursing this invisible, insubstantial state that forbade physical touch and left me unable to console the woman I loved or even to let her know I was here.

An hour passed before she made herself sit up and wipe away her tears. Resoluteness firmed her features as she straightened her spine and squared her shoulders.

"How did it fail? I did everything just as she told me!" She struck her thigh with her fist. "There must be an explanation. Maybe if I can discover what I did wrong, I can bring him back to life."

But what did you do, sweetheart? I begged. Of course, she did not hear.

Rising from the tear-soaked bed, she crossed to an ornate wooden cupboard, whose carved doors depicted a scene of elegant waterfalls and placid pools. Opening one of these doors, she stretched a hand into the shadowy interior, withdrawing the three enchanted apples I'd taken from the cyclops brothers. Also, she withdrew that deadly needle dagger, still stained with my blood.

"I must ask Patreecia," she murmured to herself.

Clutching all four items, she departed her bedchamber. Unseen, I followed. Together, we made our way through back areas of the palace, little used except by servants, and up the winding staircase of a tall, stone tower. At its top was a narrow wooden door, upon which she knocked and was bidden to enter.

Inside was a neat, tiny room, boasting a bed, a small chest of drawers, a vase of fresh flowers on the nightstand, a couple of tapestries on the walls, and—you will not believe this—an old woman spinning at a rickety spinning wheel. An old woman with shrewd black eyes, black hair nearly gone grey, clever hands, and nimble fingers. An old woman who bore a remarkable resemblance to...

Perching upon the windowsill, I folded invisible arms across my invisible chest and settled in to eavesdrop on Mercy's conversation. If my suspicions were correct, then this old woman might very well know something helpful to Mercy, just as her *twin sister* had once helped me.

Somehow, I was not even surprised to see my

Mercy had befriended both this woman and the Curator, despite their intense rivalry. If anyone could, it would be her. Also, knowing her, she had more than likely attempted to bring peace to the situation, although I supposed she must have failed, since Pelinda claimed nothing had brought peace until I killed the Curator's wolf.

"It didn't work, granny!"

Mercy fell on her knees before the old woman, burying her face in the older woman's lavender skirts.

"Didn't it? Oh no! I am sorry, my child," the old woman commiserated, ceasing her spinning and smoothing a hand over Mercy's brown-blonde hair. Her voice was remarkably similar to Pelinda the Guardian's. "Did you do exactly as I bade you?"

"I did," my beloved cried, her voice slightly muffled by the other's skirts. "Before I stabbed him, I coated the blade with juice from each apple. Afterward, I used the same blade to cut my own arm, and I allowed three drops of blood to fall on his grave. Wasn't this what you told me to do? I gave back the blood I stole!"

"Hmmm.... It was, it was." The old one ruminated a moment, then her beady black eyes brightened. Tipping Mercy's chin with a wrinkled forefinger, she peered intently into the girl's face. "But did you speak the Words of Life over him?"

"Words of Life?" Mercy straightened, dropping both the apples and the blade to the floor. "What Words of Life?" she demanded, clutching her companion's arm with both hands.

"Didn't I tell you of them? Ah, me. My memory worsens every day. It is a good thing for me your young knight slew the wolf and brought the Curator down before I forgot how to work magic altogether."

Mercy didn't bother addressing this. Instead, "What Words of Life do you mean?" she insisted. "What are they? Please, you must tell me."

"You don't know them?"

"No, don't you?" Desperation filled her eyes.

Patreecia shook her head gravely. "No, child, I do not. The Words of Life are something for you to know. In order for the spell to work, you must say the Words of Life after using the enchanted apples and giving back the stolen blood. Otherwise, the deathspell cannot be broken, and the power of the fruit will not restore him to his former state."

"But how can I say them if I don't know them?" Mercy begged.

Covering her face with her hands, she began to sob. The old woman gathered her close, patted her back gently as the princess choked, "Oh, why did he have to come? Come now? If he had delayed his sojourn in Merris even by a week, we'd never have met. Why would fate torment me like this?

"I thought when he awakened from the deathsleep, he'd be so angry with me for what I'd done that he would leave and never return. I could think of no other way to dissuade him. He simply isn't dissuadable, and I didn't have the time to try reasoning with him. I couldn't let him risk his life for mine, fighting that dragon tomorrow. But this way, after he left, I could die for my sister and my country. I could save both Buck's life and Venda's. This way, Triplehorn could claim me as his thirty-three year meal, rather than my sister.

"But now," she sobbed, "how wretchedly I've failed. I murdered Buck. I actually murdered him. I deserve to be eaten as a royal sacrifice for what I've done!"

"Hush, child, hush," old Patreecia soothed, but Mercy only wept harder, beyond any comfort.

Troubled by her mentions of tomorrow, and unable to bear the sight of her tears when I could not wipe them away, I floated out that open window. It was many stories above the cobbled courtyard below, but being a spirit did have its advantages. I felt no fear as I glided above the ground. After all, I was already dead. If there's one thing a ghost does not fear it is heights. As I wafted along over courtyard and gardens, I mulled over the scene in the tower chamber, debating what to do. It struck me that the palace library was probably quite extensive. Might some answers be hidden there, some clue as to these fabled Words of Life? I decided to find out.

CHAPTER THIRTEEN
Of Ancient Curses and Magical Volumes

I soon discovered there are some very distinct advantages to being dead, invisible, and a spirit. For one, as I've already mentioned, you needn't fear heights. Two, you can float through walls. Once I discovered this new skill, I found it so entertaining that I couldn't help gliding through the same thick, stone wall half a dozen times, as entranced by the feat as a toddler with a toy. Three, if you are of a mind to float about a castle and listen to gossip, it is easily done.

While searching for the palace library, I stopped three or four different times to overhear the servants' chatter. I gleaned some interesting information for my trouble, such as Princess Venda was generally considered—and in particular by Thresha and Delina, her serving maids—to be an absolute shrew, while Mercy was regarded with favor from the highest servant to the lowest. Everyone loved this gentle girl, who was as apt to hop up and help a servant clean up a spill as she was to make her own bed, hang up her own gowns, polish her own shoes, and help Cook Kaite in the kitchen.

The palace was buzzing like bees in a hive over the famed Sir Buckhunter Dornley coming to pay homage *to their beloved princess. Why he had left so suddenly and where he had gone was a matter of major speculation. Even more talked about than that was Mercy's impending death on the morrow. More than one maidservant I passed was sniffling and in tears. The entire staff was in a state of mourning.*

I didn't have much time.

The palace library was not difficult to find. I would have arrived much sooner had I not been of a mind to explore, eavesdrop, and also test the limits of what a ghost can and cannot do.

Once I finally reached the place, I laid aside all thoughts of delay and got straight to work. The room was huge. Floor-to-ceiling bookcases four times my height spanned the walls, crammed with books of every size, color, title, author, and subject. There was plentiful light to read or study by, both from the massive windows interspersed with the bookshelves, and the gigantic crystal chandelier lit with dozens of candles. I was more than impressed, and would have been surprised if this place was not one of Mercy's favorite haunts.

Thinking of Mercy, if I was to save her life I had to find a way to save my own first. I'd come here hoping to find a clue about the Words of Life. Not knowing where to start searching, I drifted along, several feet above the floor, until I found the section of historical works.

Ah, I thought. *Maybe there will be something*

Knight's Rebirth

useful here.

Searching through these fat tomes would have taken weeks, and I had but a single day and night. From what I gathered, Mercy was to be given to Triplehorn tomorrow. I skipped the sections dealing with Gindlon the Bold, the origins of Gindsland and other empires, and the chronicles of Merris. I knew I'd come to the right place when I found a subdivision that seemed to deal heavily with dragons and other mystical, magical, magnificent, and malevolent beasts. Well, that certainly described Triplehorn Wingback. I skimmed through titles until one caught my ghostly eye. Golden letters on its spine read, *The Curse of Merris. Or, a Dragon's Revenge.*

Aha!

Just what I needed.

Sliding the volume from its slot, I turned it over to scrutinize the cover. The title marched proudly across the top, and underneath it was an artist's fanciful rendering of a ghastly serpent with three horns on its head. I easily recognized my old foe, Triplehorn Wingback.

I opened the book to the first page, and read these words: "Herein doth follow the true account of the Curse of the kingdom of Merris, its beginning, its origin, and its commencement. Let others write what they will; this report, set down by the hand of King Villhem Frederick Merl the First, in the First Age of Gindlon the Bold, is the whole, entire, and verifiable truth."

First Age of Gindlon the Bold? Has Triplehorn really been alive that long? I wondered. *Have they really been feeding him princesses every thirty-three years for that amount of time?*

I could scarcely believe it. But after I'd settled myself on a brocade sofa and had absorbed myself for two or three hours in perusing Villhem's account, the whole idea became much more plausible.

It seemed that back when Gindlon the Bold discovered this new continent and named it after himself, he appointed thirteen of his most trustworthy generals, captains, and lieutenants to go forth and conquer the land in his name. They were each given a direction to access, and they were to map the land as they went along. That way, Gindlon could gain an idea of the shape and size of his new continent. Upon completing their task, the thirteen would then choose a parcel of land to their liking and be made its king, answerable only to the High King of Gindsland, old Gindlon himself.

One general, who would later become King Villhem Frederick Merl the First, had done quite well, had selected his parcel of land, mapped it out, and been named its king by the High King. Alas, when he returned with settlers to colonize the land, he discovered a pack of dragons had moved in during his absence, dragons who were unwilling to share their domain with humans. Villhem was no fool, and he struck a deal with the dragon leader—who was, as one might guess, none other than the famed Triplehorn Wingback. The dragons could have these mountain ranges and those cliffs, provided they left the settlers in peace and allowed King Villhem's realm to prosper.

For a time all was peaceful between the two species. Until the dragons began to prey upon the kingdom's fat, slow, and lazy oxen, cattle, horses, and sheep. Since his people could ill-afford to lose their stock, King Villhem sent emissaries to the dragon clan, begging them to go back to living upon the land. The dragons only mocked. Why bother with hunting wild game when much easier prey was at their disposal? Besides, what could these puny humans do against them anyway?

Unable to bear this insult, Villhem showed them what he could do. He waited until after the dragons had gone raiding, then gathered all of his best knights and made a sneak attack by night. Hidden in the rocks, the king and his men watched their opponents gorge themselves and then lay down to sleep.

Now, everyone knows that it takes dragons a long time to digest a meal, and when they've eaten well they sometimes sleep for days. It was the perfect time to attack, which the king and his knights did. The massacre was complete, and the king himself put a lilac colored dragonling who was less than half-grown to the sword. Perhaps if he had noticed that from her head sprouted three small, silver horns he would have let her live. However, being filled with righteous indignation, and thinking he was saving his people, Villhem slew her along with the rest.

Only one beast escaped—one who was smart enough to lie apart from his clan, one who was the proud father of that lilac dragonling, one who trembled with rage as he watched the king smite his daughter to the ground. That one dragon was Triplehorn Wingback. He did nothing that night, for his belly was full and he could scarcely move. In that condition, what could he do against so many well-armed knights? The commotion of the butchery awakened him, but he was wily enough to know he could not save his kin. He observed the slaughter from a distance, helpless.

Nevertheless, several days later when his meal had digested and he was fit to fight, Triplehorn flew straight to the palace that was being built and attacked. He took a few wounds, but there is no fighting machine more deadly than a furious, revenge-seeking, full-grown, hungry male dragon. He carved a path of death straight up to the king, but in the end decided not to kill the man. That would be far too merciful. He wanted Villhem and his descendants to suffer for their crime, just as he was suffering.

I could have guessed the rest. Every thirty-three years, for that was the number of dragons slain that terrible night by Villhem and his knights, Triplehorn would return to the kingdom of Merris. Either one of the king's daughters would be given to him to consume in retribution for the meal that kept him from defending his own offspring, or else he would wreak havoc upon the palace, the capital city, and the realm in general.

Needless to say, in all the centuries since those days, Triplehorn's demand had never been refused. If a princess was not available, the next lady in closest kinship to the king was offered. In his account, Villhem reminded those who would rule after him that, even though this sacrifice pained their hearts, they must remember a king's foremost task is the guardianship of his people. Therefore, it was better that one royal maiden die than an entire kingdom be destroyed.

I may have had no real stomach to speak of, yet after reading this I felt sickened as I considered all those poor young princesses like Mercy's aunt who'd met their fate paying for a sin with which they'd had nothing to do. Princesses, many of whom were undoubtedly just as brave and generous and loving as my Mercy.

How could they do that? How could a father willingly send his daughter to be eaten by a dragon? Were he any kind of man he would take up arms and slay the beast or die trying.

The old Curator in the forest had been right. There was a great deal of hidden danger in this kingdom. Furthermore, he'd been entirely correct to call King Merl a coward, for coward he was: a craven coward of the worst sort. Nobody but a sniveling coward would allow his child to be eaten without at least *trying* to prevent it! I knew, were I in Merl's place, that was exactly what I would do, trained knight or not.

My opinion of my beloved's father and his ancestors could not have been lower, but I hadn't the time to dwell on his shortcomings. Instead, I drifted from the couch over to the vacant spot on the bookshelf and slid Villhem's volume back into it. I now knew the secret behind Mercy's horrendous destiny, but that wouldn't help me save her.

Again I fell to searching shelves, bypassing more historical sections, then philosophical, then scientific, then political. At last, in a dark corner of the chamber where scant sun and candlelight reached, I discovered a small division of books which seemed to deal with magic, spells, potions, and other mystical pursuits.

Could help be found here?

While running my hand over spine after spine, considering and rejecting titles as irrelevant to my search, my invisible fingers chanced to slide over a red leather volume tucked in amongst the rest. There was no name on the spine. I would have paid it no heed, except for the fact that, as my ghostly fingers brushed it, a voice in my head suddenly spoke up.

Take me out. Open me. Read me. I can help you. What the deuce?

Do it, the voice insisted. *You know you want to. Take me out, invisible knight. I can help you, I promise.*

Hesitantly, I reached out and touched the nameless volume. Was this what was speaking to me?

Thou art an oaf! the little voice declared impatiently. *Take me out, take me out, take me out!*

"Fine!" I snapped. It was the book speaking to me! But amazing as that was, I still did not like it ordering me about. Before I did what it wanted, I told it (and since I was a ghost my voice could only be heard in my own head), "I will only take you out if you promise to speak more politely. Who are you to command me?"

Who are you to reject the demands of magic? returned the book. *I can help you, but only if you take me out. We haven't much time, you know.*

"How can you help me?" I asked as I slid it out and opened its cover. Inside, the pages were—"You're blank!" I snarled. "How can you possibly help me when your pages are blank?"

I can help you, Sir Oaf, because I have lived in this section of the library for more years than you've been alive, the book answered. *I've had time to become acquainted with all the other books on this shelf, and I know which ancient volume has the information you seek.*

"What information?" I was suspicious. "How

does a rude little book come to know so much?"

Inside my head, I heard a longsuffering sigh. *Because I am magic, you stupid oaf. Gracious, what does an extraordinary woman like Mercy see in you? I was created with magic, I exist by magic. I know things by magic, and I am speaking to you with magic. If you have not figured this out by now, you really are denser than you appear.*

"How do you know how I appear? I'm invisible."

There! Let the little beast wrangle his way out of that one.

Not to me, you're not, answered the object smugly. *I am magic, remember? I can see you perfectly well.*

Apparently, the wretch had an answer for everything.

Let us not fuss, it said. *You have rescued me from countless years of boredom by picking me up, so I will help you, just as I promised. But in return, you must do me a favor.*

"What sort of favor?" I inquired suspiciously, unsure I wanted anything to do with a know-it-all magical book, even if it did claim it could help me find the powerful Words of Life.

A good one, assured the book. *I want you to take me and write in me.*

"Write what? I haven't the time to sit around writing stories, and I've certainly no ink and quill at hand."

Not that sort of writing, oaf. And you needn't make up anything. What I want is for you to fill my pages with a unique story—yours. You are the famous Sir Buckhunter Dornley. You have lived many an adventure, unless I am entirely mistaken. Would that we had the time and pages to write them all. However, this latest adventure is surely your greatest. Wouldn't you agree?

"I suppose."

No supposition about it, protested the book. *You know I am right. It is a tale worthy of being remembered, and I want it to be memorialized. I want you to start at the very beginning of this tale, and fill my pages with the story of how your life has been changed of late. For that is my enduring magic: I change lives. I will change yours now, by giving you the information you seek. And, should you do as you're told and record your story in me, I promise it will not only be a lasting tribute to you and your princess, but an enduring memorial to the life-changing power of love.*

It wasn't such a bad idea after all, I admitted gruffly. Maybe this was a story worth being retold and remembered. My life had certainly been changed while living it. No denying that. If my story had the power to change other lives, shouldn't I tell it?

"Very well, master book," I finally agreed. "I will record my story from beginning to end. But I cannot do it now. I haven't the time to be sitting about writing, and—"

Oh, you blockhead, you fool! exclaimed the book. *Do you understand anything at all? I am a magical book! You do not write in me using ordinary ink and quill. You use your mind, your thoughts, the words in your head.*

"The words in my hea—"

Yes, that's it! the volume snapped. *At last, you begin to understand. All you must do is think a sentence, and it will appear on the first page of my*

Knight's Rebirth

book. Try it, try it, urged the book.

"But I've many thoughts running through my head," I protested. "How will I sort out which ones I want written down and which ones I don't? After all, I do not want to set down just anything."

Never you mind, reassured my odd companion. *I will see to that. Go ahead and try it, Sir Knight. Think of your opening sentence. Try it!*

Screwing up my invisible face, I tried to visualize myself sitting down at a desk and chair, a clean sheet of parchment, an inkstand, and a quill before me. Dipping the quill in ink, I would hold it over the page. What would I write, right now at this instant, if that was where I was and what I was doing?

In a flash, it came to me.

My name is Buckhunter Dornley, I would write, *and I am dead.*

To my amazement, just as the brash little volume had promised, neat, precise, handwritten letters popped up on its opening page.

"My name is Buckhunter Dornley," they said, "and I am dead."

You see how easy that was? crowed the book. *Not all magic is difficult. Now your story can be continued at your leisure. You think it, and I will see that it is set down. Furthermore, you needn't carry me about with you, for now that your first thought is recorded, we are linked. Put me back in my spot, and even from there I shall hear and write your story. But remember, do come back for me when all is finished. I should very much like to see your princess's face when she sees what you have found.*

In spite of myself, I smiled. "Yes, Mercy will love you," I told it sincerely.

As soon as I said it, the amusement faded. Speaking Mercy's name had brought her predicament to mind.

"Master book, do not forget our bargain. You said you knew where I must search for the answers I seek. I've already begun to fulfill my part of the agreement. Will you now fulfill yours?"

Naturally! replied my friend, the book. *I am happy to assist. If you will pull down that large purple book—yes, the one three shelves above your head—you will find a reference to the powerful Words of Life. Is that not what you seek?*

"It is indeed," I answered, stowing my friend away and reaching up for the volume it had indicated. "It is indeed."

I left the library later, the final pieces of the puzzle having fallen into place, including the one that Mercy did not have. She may not have known the words of life, but I did. Now, I simply had to find some way to approach her and share what I'd learned. When she spoke the magical phrases over me, I would be saved.

Just as importantly, I had to think of some way to save her from Triplehorn, who was coming tomorrow to claim his thirty-three year prize. Second in line to the throne, that sacrifice would be Mercy, unless I could prevent it. No one else was going to fight for her. That only left me, dead or not. Pelinda's secret would certainly help; how could I use it to my

Knight's Rebirth

greatest advantage?

For hours, I drifted aimlessly over the Kingdom of Merris, pondering these matters. Dawn brought both the sun and a restless, undeniable urge to return to my body's lonely grave in the forest. Unable to resist, I obeyed, although I wasn't sure what was happening to me. Once I arrived, I felt my invisible spirit being pulled under the earth...and back into my corpse. I gasped as breath returned, opened my eyes, and discovered myself encased in a plain pine box. There was little room to wriggle about, yet I managed to grasp my dagger which I then used to pry open the lid of the crude coffin. Thank goodness they'd buried me with my weapons. This also made digging my way out of the thin layer of soil covering the coffin much easier.

As soon as I emerged from the bowels of the earth I knew I hadn't been fully restored. The stench of death clung to me, and I felt weaker than I'd ever felt before. Still, I managed to steal carefully through the trees, make it to the palace stables, and slip past the sleeping guards. There, I retrieved Stalker and the rest of my belongings, which I found stashed in an empty stall, probably for later disposal. Collecting these, I crept away again before I could be noticed.

Back in the trees bordering the palace grounds, I donned my armor. It was a slow and painful process, but I needed to cover my rotting flesh and moldering skin. Although I hadn't been in the grave long enough to decay, I was anyway. Something about the magic Mercy used when she killed me must have produced these odd side effects.

First, it had temporarily freed my spirit from my flesh, but not from this world. Second, it had brought my spirit back to my body, but had failed to restore my life as I'd previously known it. Essentially, I was a walking corpse, but I was not about to give up. Dawn meant tomorrow had arrived. Half-dead or not, I was going to rescue the woman I loved, and let no power in this life or the next try to stop me

CHAPTER FOURTEEN
Of Dragons Secrets and Dragons Toes

Thus we return to the beginning of the tale, where I was sitting on Stalker's back, awaiting my turn to enter the lists. You remember, do you not? Let us return there now, and pick up this story from where it started.

Sir Derick of Greyford, the false name I'd given to the tournament herald, was eventually called. With a final glance at my brave princess, I gathered Stalker's reins firmly in one fist and hefted my lance in the other. A nudge to my warhorse's flanks, and we trotted out proudly to take the field, preparing to meet our opponent: a slender knight with a yellow plume on his helmet and a blue bull on his shield.

My muscles were quivering. The sun was too hot. The more I sweated, the worse I stank. The mingled odors of sweat and decay were enough to choke me, but with sheer willpower I forced aside any awareness save that of going into battle.

We lined up at opposite ends of the jousting field, on either side of the wooden divider between us. For a breathtaking moment, perfect stillness reigned. Then the scarf was dropped, fluttering lightly to the earth. I raised my lance and so did my opponent. Our horses sprang forward and we charged one another. A second or two passed, and we met with a crash in the midst of the field. Weakened or not, my skills as a knight were unmatched. I knew the exact spot to aim my blow. The strategy worked as beautifully as it always did. My opponent toppled from his saddle, leaving me the winner of that match.

And the next.

And the next.

And the next.

I triumphed in four successive matches, leaving me the undisputed master of the field.

For you, Mercy, I thought, wheeling Stalker around and guiding him towards the royal pavilion wherein sat King Merl, his lovely queen, and his two daughters. There I halted, waiting to dismount until the king and his family had descended the makeshift stairs and approached. When they stood before me, with Mercy holding a velvet cushion in her hands, upon which lay a golden dragon figurine—the prize for winning the tournament—I clambered slowly, carefully off my mount. Stalker shied nervously, uncomfortable with my unfamiliar scent, but I calmed him with a pat to the muzzle.

Stepping past his nose, I bowed stiffly and awkwardly, like an old man, before the king. At that instant, a fresh, northerly breeze blew my offensive stench right into the faces of the royal family. Both

Knight's Rebirth

Princess Venda and her mother covered their noses with silk handkerchiefs, turning their heads to cough. King Merl pulled a terrible face. Mercy alone, over whom I towered as I straightened, made no show of disgust. Too sweet for any sort of rudeness, she smiled bravely, although her face had gone chalk white. I don't know if it was from my rank odor, or the knowledge that the event honoring her was at an end—meaning she'd soon be facing the vicious jaws of a dragon. Pale or not, she still inched closer, raising the pillow.

"As the one for whom this tournament has been held," she stated formally, "I offer you my gratitude for your efforts, Sir Knight. You have more than proven your valor and your courage. I now proclaim you the undisputed champion of today's events. I hope you will accept this unworthy trophy as a testament to your gallantry."

"Thank you, Princess," I said gently, relieved that she would be hard pressed to recognize my croaking, raspy voice, "but I have far more in mind as recompense than a golden statuette."

Ignoring her shock, I turned to the king.

"Your Majesty," I began, offering him an unsteady bow, "may I say that I am not unaware of the real reason for this tournament? Rather than accept this golden dragon, I would claim as my prize the honor of fighting Triplehorn Wingback for the life of the princess."

Gasps arose from each member of the royal family, as well as the servants, courtiers, and noblemen gathered close enough to hear.

"What? Of what are you speaking? Who are you?" the king blustered angrily.

"Throughout my travels in this kingdom," I went on calmly, "I have learned the ill-kept secret of the dragon who returns every thirty-three years to claim a princess as his sacrifice. If the maiden is not yielded, he threatens to wreak great havoc upon the kingdom of Merris. Thus, the princess has never been denied him." Pausing, I peered straight at Mercy through the narrow slits of my visor. "I would not have that be your daughter's fate."

Mercy's pretty lips parted in surprise. Her sapphire eyes sought mine, but I hastily turned my head, lest she somehow identify me and foil my plan.

"You truly wish to fight Triplehorn Wingback for Mercy's life?" the queen breathed through the folds of her delicate hankie.

"I claim that right as my prize for winning the tournament held in her honor," I replied, my steady gaze fixed upon the king. "Your Majesty cannot deny me."

Swallowing hard, the king shook his head. "Nay, I cannot. Honor will not allow it. But...what if you fail?"

I shrugged. My knees were growing weaker by the second, and if I did not remount Stalker soon, I didn't think I would be able to do so again. "Then the princess will die, just as she has been fated since birth. However, if I win," I warned sternly, "I also claim another right of the victor: I claim your daughter as my wife."

More cries of astonishment from those around us. Even Mercy was shocked enough to retreat a step. "My very great thanks for this honor, Sir Knight, but I cannot wed you. My heart belongs to another."

"And where might he be?" I inquired boldly,

returning my attention to her. "You love a man, and he does not love you enough to fight for you?"

Tears glistened in her eyes and her chin trembled with grief. "He would," she asserted staunchly, "but cannot. He is dead."

A thrill of happiness shot through my veins, quickening me. Not only did her heart belong to me, but she fully believed that, had I lived, I would be fighting for her. Her faith was enough. It gave me the strength to carry on.

"Then he must have been a worthy man, both to have won your heart and to face a dragon for you," I conceded, dipping my head to her. "I envy him."

Before she could say anything else, I readdressed her father. "I have won the tournament and claimed my prize. What say you, Your Majesty?"

In the end, despite Mercy's quiet protests that she would not have me risk my life, and that she could hardly marry me when she loved another, her father had no choice but to acquiesce. His word was given: Mercy would be mine if I overcame the dragon. With some difficulty I turned and managed to remount my horse. I didn't bother with any farewell speech that might betray my affection and thus my identity. Instead, I stole one final glance at the woman I loved, wheeled Stalker about, and trotted off towards the massive rock quarry just off the tournament grounds where my old enemy, Triplehorn Wingback, eagerly awaited his next royal meal.

Stalker stepped carefully down the pencil-thin path leading into the ancient rock quarry. The stones for Merris's castle had been mined from this place, and it now made a perfect dragon pit. When we reached the sandy floor, Triplehorn was curled up and fast asleep, but the tremors of Stalker's heavy hooves roused him. His hooded yellow eyes cracked, blinked once or twice, then rolled towards us. By the time we stood a dozen paces away, my sword drawn and ready, he had raised his horned snout. Sharp, white fangs protruded from both his upper and lower lip. With a sneer of sheer hatred, he fixed those ugly reptilian eyes upon the two of us.

"What'sss thisss?" he hissed, his red forked tongue flicking in and out as he spoke. "My old nemesssisss, Sssir Buckhunter Dornley?"

So he, unlike the royal family, had recognized my horse. When I'd crept back into the palace grounds to claim my armor, I'd taken pains to steal a different shield from a palace guardsman so no one would see my emblem and figure out my identity. I'd briefly considered stealing a different warhorse, but the risk was much higher, and I had no interest in going into battle without Stalker, my old battle companion. Instead of a whole new horse, I had taken care to drape him in a different caparison that I'd snatched. Had Mercy or her father been paying closer attention, they might have recognized Stalker's head and face, but they were so wrapped up in their own grief that they'd failed to give the big destrier a second look.

"What a pleasssant sssurprissse," the dragon jeered, pushing himself up on his hind legs to sit on his rather impressive haunches. The tufted end of his long, serpent tail flicked menacingly against the quarry's dirt floor. "You are no princccesss, but I can asss readily devour you asss she."

"Think again, dragon," I snapped. "You'll devour no one this day. I've come to fight for the woman I love. I'll see you dead before you see her in that condition."

Unperturbed, Triplehorn swung his head mockingly from side to side. "Sssir Buckhunter Dornley finally brought down by a woman? The woman dessstined to be my next meal? How amusssing." He parted thin lizard lips in a hideous smile, revealing two impressive rows of elongated, pointy teeth. "Today I shall devour both my old foe and hisss new love."

"Today, you will have no human meals," I snarled.

Refusing to trade idle taunts and insults with the beast a second longer, I put heels to my horse's side and charged. Triplehorn reared back in surprise, flapping his gigantic, leathery wings, trying to lift himself into the air. It was an old maneuver, one I knew well. In the air, a dragon is nimble and swift, able to weave in and out, back and forth, and up and down with frightening dexterity. It is well-nigh impossible to bring one down from the air, for it takes all a knight's skill to simply defend himself from aerial assaults, especially when he's armed with only a sword instead of a lance or a longbow.

Fortunately, Triplehorn Wingback was not a fire-breather. With those breeds, all a knight can do is hide in a secure place and shoot arrows, or else attempt a sneak attack. The best strategy is to slay the dragon while it is off guard, or the knight is no better than kindling. I'd killed one or two fire-breathers in my day, and I don't think it's unmanly of me to admit I hoped never to face another.

At any rate, Triplehorn may not have been a fire-breather, but he was a wily as they come. The last two times we'd fought, he'd been unable to overcome my excellent swordsmanship and skill with the lance, and couldn't get close enough to inflict any serious damage. Since he'd been in the air while I was earthbound, I hadn't been able to get close enough to inflict any serious damage on him, either. Consequently, we'd battled to a draw, which ended with Triplehorn flying off, swearing vengeance another day.

Today, I had a new plan, built off the secret Pelinda had shared with me in her forest cottage. In fact, as a part of this plan, I'd purposefully left my lance at the tournament field. Triplehorn saw this, and had foolishly let me get too close. It was a fatal mistake. This time, when I charged, I didn't aim for his soft underbelly or his flexible throat, as I might have before. Those were the places he must defend and was expecting me to attack. Thanks to Pelinda and her magical wheel, this time I went for an area far more vulnerable.

I went for his toes.

Now, it is common knowledge that dragons love nothing better than gathering vast treasure troves and hoarding them in caves. What isn't so commonly known is that with every third heap of treasure a male dragon collects, they magically grow another toe. Some older males who are expert treasure gatherers have been known to develop as many as seven or eight toes, rather than the standard three. As you can imagine, extra toes are a great source of pride in the dragon culture. They are also especially important during mating season, helping the male dragon win the lady of his choice, but I digress.

The point is, male dragons are terribly fond of their toes, and go to great pains to protect these valuable assets. Triplehorn, old treasure thief that he was, boasted five toes on each foot, of which he was excessively proud. He was also unaware that I knew anything about the importance of those toes, and I wouldn't have, if not for Patreecia's twin sister in Dead Derion. But since I knew, I intended to make good use of the information.

As I've said, the dragon was flapping his wings mightily to lift himself into the air, but because he'd let me get too close, he wasn't quick enough. By the time I reached him on the run, he was high enough overhead that I couldn't harm his belly or neck, but I could reach his toes. Too bad for him. I thrust my blade upwards, driving it directly into the third toe on his right foot. Screaming in pain, the old serpent dropped right out of the sky, falling with a crash that shook the earth. He twisted over on his back, writhing in snakelike fashion, filling the air with the most horrendous, twisted shrieks you've ever heard. I felt no pity for him.

"My toesss, my toesss!" screamed the monster, forked tongue flicking wildly in and out of his jaws. "What have you done? Oh cruel, cruel knight. My toesss!"

Dismounting carefully from Stalker's back, I gripped my bloody sword tightly in both hands as I lurched up to the dragon. With a dodge to avoid his massive, flailing tail, I rammed my blade into the largest toe on his left foot and pinned it to the dusty ground. I'd never heard such wailing. Of course, few people understand the ancient language of dragons, so his sniveling over his cherished toes would've meant nothing to them. I, however, had formed an acquaintance with dragon talk throughout the years, and for Mercy's sake enjoyed every one of the creature's howls.

For good measure, I stabbed yet another toe with my dagger, before removing my sword from the pinned toe. For such a mighty beast, Triplehorn was now a blubbering mess. Stalking up the dragon's head, I planted my boot on his neck. My sword was poised to pierce his vulnerable throat.

"Silence, dragon!" I commanded, bearing all the weight of my corpse upon him.

A wave of weakness assailed me, forcing me to close my eyes and draw several deep breaths before I could go on. That was alright, though, because it gave Triplehorn a moment to reduce his yowls to pitiful sniffles and whimpers.

Still feeling not the slightest speck of pity, I bent closer and looked him right in his devilish yellow eyes. "You see I've finally bested you," I ground out. "I've injured three of your precious toes, and if you don't do precisely as I say, I shall slice off the rest."

A fat, shiny dragon tear rolled down his scaly green cheek. "What would you have me do?" he blubbered.

CHAPTER FIFTEEN
Of Renewals, Rebirths, and Happy Endings

If you've never flown on the back of a dragon, I can tell you it's quite a ride. That something so enormous can lift itself so easily and dart through the air is nothing short of amazing. Soaring through the sky on leathery wings evokes a feeling of freedom like nothing else. As I sped towards a final conclusion of all these events, hopefully a happy one, I prayed that freedom was indeed about to be found. Freedom for Mercy from this ancient curse. Freedom for me from this state of living death.

Only Mercy could save me. I had rescued her from a dragon. Could she rescue me, in turn?

When Triplehorn and I alighted gracefully on the tournament field before the royal pavilion, all but the hardiest folk screamed and fled, certain the monster had either come to claim Mercy or to slaughter everyone in his path. He was a fearsome sight, I'll admit, being taller than the royal box and covered with emerald green scales that shimmered to olive with the slightest of movements. Blood covered his toes, yet the proud lizard lifted his serpentine head grandly. His silver horns caught, reflected the sunlight. He put on a very brave show, thrashing his thick tail and roaring a challenge to the few guardsmen who dared approached with spears clenched in trembling hands. The roar was enough to send them fleeing in terror, running away so fast and so far that to this day I don't believe they've been found.

With the greatest of difficulty I put on my own brave front, clambering off Triplehorn's high back, stepping onto his upraised knee, and swinging off it to the ground. Clasping the hilt of my sword, I affected a swagger to hide the weakness in my knees as I strode up to the king and his family. Their backs were pressed to the varnished paneling of the royal box, and they eyed both the dragon and myself with their mouths rounded into perfect O's.

"I have returned, Your Highness, having subdued the dragon as promised." I swept a gauntleted hand towards Triplehorn. He glowered, but kept his end of the bargain and did nothing to retaliate. "I would ask you, Sire, to now fulfill your word by giving me your daughter's hand in marriage—the daughter whose life I have saved," I added hastily, not wanting to risk another mix up in identity. "And only if the princess will consent."

King Merl glanced helplessly at his queen, his eldest daughter, and then at Mercy, who lifted her chin bravely and stepped forward.

Knight's Rebirth

"Indeed, you have my eternal gratitude, Sir Knight," she said, casting an anxious glance at the beast that had planned to devour her. "Were matters not as they are, I would be honored to wed such a noble knight. However, are you certain you wish to marry me? I think it only fair to remind you that my heart belongs to another man. I'll not hold you to your promise if you wish to forgo it."

Suddenly, I could stand it no longer. There she stood, the woman I loved, as beautiful as a summer sunrise, plucky and sweet, gracious, kind, and proclaiming her love for me before one and all.

"Mercy," I cried, falling heavily to my knees, unable to maintain the deception any longer. "Mercy, sweetheart, don't you know me? Don't you recognize me, my love?"

"Buck?" Her hands flew to her mouth. The color in her cheeks drained, leaving her face a sickly shade of white. "Buck, can it be? Is...is that you?" she faltered, advancing a few hesitant steps.

"It is me," I replied, lifting my gauntleted hands. She took them, clutching them tightly in her own, scanning the slits of my helmet, trying desperately to see my eyes.

"Impossible," she whispered, her gaze darting back and forth. "You—you're dead! You were buried. I saw all this, I—"

"True," I agreed. "I am dead...yet I am not. Remove my helmet and see," I offered, although inwardly I quailed to think of Mercy beholding the monster I was now.

Licking her lips nervously, she released my hands to place her palms on either side of the helmet. One swift tug and it was gone. Her horror couldn't be contained. She dropped the heavy piece, stumbling backwards.

"Oh Buck, what have I done?" she gasped. "Dearest, what have I done?"

Bless her soul, I knew then how much she truly loved me when she dropped to her knees to throw her arms around my foul-smelling corpse and pull me close. How she could bear to touch me or urge my rotting face into the hollow of her neck I will never know, but that's exactly what she did. Maybe love makes one brave, or indifferent. Whatever the case, she ran a dainty hand over my stringy grey hair, saying, "You saved my life and I destroyed yours. Oh, what have I done? What have I done?"

"Don't cry, Mercy," I murmured against her skin, holding her as firmly as my weak, trembling arms would allow. "Hope yet remains. Speak the Words of Life over me and I'll be restored."

"But how?" she said through tears, leaning back in my arms so she could see my face. Triplehorn, her family, and the growing crowd of spectators had been forgotten. For her, I was the only person in the world, just as she was for me. "How, Buck?" she insisted desperately. "How can I say them when I don't know them?"

I smiled, and I'm sure it was a hideous sight, since my gums were black and my few remaining teeth were rotting and yellow. Mercy didn't seem to notice. "You do know them, my love," I assured her. "Remember when we first met? How you found me in the forest and thought me dead? Remember what you said?

"More importantly," I went on, framing her smooth cheeks with nearly skeletal hands, "think of

Knight's Rebirth

how you made me whole the first time. Think of how you and you alone truly brought me to life."

A tear dripped down her cheek. Catching it with a half-rotted thumb, I wiped it tenderly away. "*You*, Mercy. Your happiness and your love made me live for the first time in my life. Speak the Words of Life over me—command me to come back to life. Tell me you love me, and it will be enough."

What a pathetic picture: a corpse in armor pleading with a velvet-gowned, golden-crowned princess to say that she loved him. But do you know what? That velvet-gowned, golden-crowned princess *did* love him, and she proved it by leaning close and brushing her soft, warm lips against his dry, peeling dead ones.

"Whether you are sleeping or dead, I do not know," she whispered in my ear, "but I command you to awaken and come back to life. You must do so because I am the princess of this land, and you will obey me." This time, rather than slap my face, she stole a kiss—of which I was more than happy to be robbed—before adding, "What is more, I love you, Sir Buckhunter Dornley. And if you will not return to life for any other reason, return for this: that I love you and need you. That I cannot live without you." Her eyes were liquid jewels. "Come back to me."

As the final syllable rolled off her tongue, I felt a shiver start at the tips of my toes, race up my calves and thighs and into my stomach. Onward it sped, up my spine, the back of my neck, and into my head, where it burst into a riot of sensation and color. The ground shifted, tilting sideways. Mercy's image wavered wildly, forcing me to shut my eyes. From somewhere distant I heard a woman scream in alarm, while a man shouted, "Look! Look, he is changing!"

Indeed I was, changing before their very eyes. Flesh ripened on my bones like fruit on a tree. My skin knit together, and my hair regained its normal color and texture. I felt my strength replenishing even as the rank odor of death was blown away by a fresh, stiff breeze. Through it all, Mercy held onto me, refusing to let go. Her strength was all I had, all I'd ever had. I swayed and would have fallen, except for her arms around me. Stars, galaxies, and comets danced before my closed eyes. An eternity was lived in those few seconds, and when those overwhelming sensations finally diminished, I opened my eyes to behold my princess's face.

"Mercy," I breathed, but she gave me no time to say anything else. With a cry of sheer happiness she flew at me, throwing herself into my arms so forcefully that even her slight weight knocked me off balance. I had to catch us by throwing out a hand, bracing it behind me. She pressed her mouth to mine, and it clear stole my breath, along with every lucid thought in my head. All around us, people began to cheer, to laugh, and some of the women to weep for joy.

"Praise be! My daughter will live, and my kingdom is saved," Mercy's father shouted.

Even grumpy old Triplehorn added his own approval. "Very niccce," the dragon hissed.

Oblivious, I took no notice of anything save the feel of the woman I loved clasped close with one arm, her mouth against mine, and the happy tears on her cheeks wetting my own. It was one of those flawless moments never to be forgotten, one I would recall often for the rest of my days. By her courage, her love,

Knight's Rebirth

Mercy of Merris had brought me to life, slain me, then brought me back again. I had thought to rescue her from a dragon, but, in the end, she had rescued me. Today was not merely the day of a dead knight's rebirth, but the rebirth of myself as a better human being. As a better man.

We were joined in marriage that very day by my bride's father. I still had not forgiven King Merl for not moving to rescue his daughter, but he was the highest authority in the land, and when he offered to marry us neither Mercy nor I could refuse. That day, I claimed Mercy as my wife and still consider her the greatest prize I've ever won. More than any ladies' favors (I had to give away my latest collection quickly, as I was now a happily married man), more than any fat purses of gold and silver, more than all the glory, fame, and honor in the world, my wife had been worth fighting—and dying—for.

The throne of Merris eventually went to Lady Venda and the snooty, selfish princeling she married, but we did not mind. Rumor had it that the two quarreled constantly, for in a marriage of two such likeminded, self-centered people how can there be peace? Once, I thought of using that inner turmoil as an excuse to lay claim to the kingdom, using Triplehorn to back me, but Mercy talked me out of it.

"No, darling," she reproved, laying a hand on my sleeve. "We wouldn't be happy as king and queen, living in a stuffy palace surrounded by stuffy servants, with a host of stuffy duties to perform. That is not the life for us. You know it is not."

As always, she was right.

There was nothing stuffy about marriage to Mercy. I may have given up dragon hunting and killing cyclopes, but I exchanged those adventures for the adventure of being married to the most unpredictable princess in all of Gindsland. As Mercy had always wanted to do, as she now had time to do, she visited the most esteemed cooking schools in the realm while I competed in tournaments. Being a knight was too much in my blood to give it up altogether, just as perfecting her craft was in hers. I will say that when Stalker and I competed in those tournaments, I now wore and accepted no woman's favors except my wife's.

In time, another new birth came of Mercy's and my union. A little girl with Mercy's blonde-brown hair and my grey eyes came to us in the springtime. I can honestly say holding my daughter in my arms for the first time was the proudest moment of my life. The satisfaction of winning tournaments was nothing compared to the honor of holding the first child my wife had given me.

Even Triplehorn Wingback, who I had finally bested, got a happy ending. After I made him revoke his ancient curse and renounce all rights to future Merris princesses, he left the kingdom for good. I wasn't sorry to see him go, but I must confess, now that the heat of battle had faded, there was the tiniest spot of warmth in my heart for the old serpent. Being a father myself, I could sympathize with the agony of watching his adored daughter die and being helpless to prevent it. That's not to say I approved of his method of revenge, but I could understand why he was driven to seek vengeance.

Anyway, as to the happy part, I've heard that his toes healed quite nicely, and just in time for mating season. A lovely female dragon with scales of gold and wings of scarlet has been spotted at Triplehorn's new treasure cave, and between them I believe they've hatched a half-dozen dragonlings of green, gold, and red. All with impressive silver horns, of course. And that is certainly a far better ending for a dragon than devouring a human princess every thirty-three years.

Thus, I close my tale in a much happier fashion than it was begun. Perhaps we had to travel through fire and water to find peace, yet happiness waited around the bend and the journey was worth every step of the way. As a final, fitting inscription to this magical little volume, the story of my life, death, and rebirth, I will only say that I hope you, my reader, may likewise find the joy you seek. Then, as with my Mercy and I, it can be said of you—

"And they lived happily ever after."

The End

Dear Reader,

Thank you so much for giving me your time and attention with this book! *Knight's Rebirth* was actually one of the first short stories I ever wrote many years ago. During the next few years, I expanded it into a novella, then this book you see here. Being one of my initial works, it's always held a special place in my heart, and I hope it's touched yours.

Speaking of firsts, did you know the first book I ever had published was actually a volume of poetry? *A Minstrel's Musings* debuted in 2009 from Cyberwizard Productions. At the time I was really into poetry, and didn't foresee how prose would eventually take over my writing. However, I still love poetry, and as a little bonus for you I thought I'd include a special poem from *A Minstrel's Musings* here in *Knight's Rebirth*. Believe it or not, I didn't actually have Mercy of Merris in mind when I wrote this poem, but it seems fitting to her and Buck's story. I hope you enjoy it.

If you have enjoyed this work, stay tuned for a sneak peek at one of my other books, *Aerisia: Land Beyond the Sunset*. This is the first book in my *Sunset Lands Beyond* trilogy which, although not fairytale inspired like *Knight's Rebirth*, certainly has plenty of fairytale elements. Also check out its companion series, *Beyond the Sunset Lands*, which is still in progress. If more fairytales are your speed, I currently have two original fairytales published in free anthologies—"The Hero of Emoh" in *Hall of Heroes*, and "The Princess and the Stone-Picker" in *Tales of Ever After*.

Sarah Ashwood

If you feel led to leave a review of *Knight's Rebirth* and let me know what you think, I'd greatly appreciate it. Also, my bio, my website, my newsletter sign up, and my social media links are all listed at the back of this book. I love hearing from my readers! Lastly, I found some simply amazing images on Pinterest that helped craft the final version of this book. If you'd care to see them, you can check out my *Knight's Rebirth* <u>board</u>. Have fun!

Until next time—

Sarah

MERCY
By Sarah Ashwood

When *Mercy* brought me to that shore
I thought me home, to seek no more
When I awoke, not bound—but free
I thought it meant a changed me

Alas, she tricked me and deceived
A fool, was I, to have believed
Until I realized—slow to learn—
That *Mercy* did my heart discern

In my soul, she'd found scant grace
And so ignored my tear-stained face
Because I pled for only me
While all the rest forgot to see

Withholding grace, she sought to teach
That others, beyond me, I should reach
That fellow human weal and woe,
Pain and love, I ought to know

So *Mercy* taught me this great sooth
That hope and faith and love and truth
If used by humans, one and all
Can break down barriers, like a wall

Now upon a gleaming shore
With *Mercy's* aid, I've passed that door
And in the sunlight think I see
What it means to be set free

*Originally published in "A Minstrel's Musings" by Cyberwizard Productions, April 2009.

ABOUT THE AUTHOR

Don't believe all the hype. Sarah Ashwood isn't really a gladiator, a Highlander, a fencer, a skilled horsewoman, an archer, a magic wielder, or a martial arts expert. That's only in her mind. In real life, she's a genuine Okie from Muskogee, who grew up in the wooded hills outside the oldest town in Oklahoma and holds a B.A. in English from American Military University. She now lives (mostly) quietly at home with her husband and three sons, where she tries to sneak in a daily run or workout to save her sanity and keep her mind fresh for her next story.

To keep up to date with Sarah's work and new releases, sign up for her newsletter. You can also visit her website, www.sarahashwoodauthor.com, follow her on Bookbub, or find her on Facebook, Pinterest, Instagram, and Twitter.

WORKS BY SARAH ASHWOOD

THE SUNSET LANDS BEYOND TRILOGY

Aerisia: Land Beyond the Sunset
Aerisia: Gateway to the Underworld
Aerisia: Field of Battle

BEYOND THE SUNSET LANDS SERIES (IN PROGRESS)

Aerisian Refrain (now available)
Aerisian Waning (forthcoming)
Aerisian Nightfall (forthcoming)
Aerisian Dawn (forthcoming)

NOVELLAS

Amana

SHORT WORKS

"The Hero of Emoh" in *Hall of Heroes*
"The Princess and the Stone-Picker" in *Tales of Ever After*
"Lost" in *Like a Woman*

AERISIA
Land Beyond the Sunset

By Sarah Ashwood

Prophecy of the Artan

She is of our world and beyond. From another place, another time, she will come. She carries the burden of tomorrow, and her true essence will be birthed with the moon and the dawn. The Singing Stones once more will sing, and she shall unite those long hated with those who long have feared them. Unity with the everlasting will heal her soul, lifting the eternal from rejection and fear. She will be untouched by man and untainted by The Evil. In her will be met all the Powers of Good, and with them shall she defeat The Evil. The Dark Powers she shall overcome by becoming, yet not. Bound to the past, the bond will be broken that she may pass through the vales of shadow and despair to walk forevermore in the light. Wars may rage, kingdoms rise and fall, and monarchs topple, but the Artan will defend her people. Aerisia by her strength will be kept, and in her time peace will prosper.

Wealth, power, fame, status, notoriety, prestige. Magic.

Some people spend their whole lives chasing these dreams. Others purposefully avoid them. Me, I neither sought nor shunned them, but they came to me anyway, unasked and unwanted.

Why?

Because others believe what I do not. Others see me as somebody I don't know. They want me to become this person, but how can I do that when I'm not even sure she exists? If I'm wrong and she actually does exist, how can I discover her? How can I become her? When you've been ordinary your entire life, it possible to reinvent yourself into someone you've never met, never known, never even heard of before? Someone from history? Someone from legend? Someone from prophecy?

Someone with magic?

CHAPTER ONE
Mysterious Stranger

"Hannah, what are you doing? Why are you just standing around? They'll be here in a little over an hour."

My older sister's voice was tight with frustration. She lowered a stack of plates to the dining room table more forcefully than the delicate china deserved. I winced to see our mother's treasured dishes treated that way, but, thankfully, nothing was broken.

"Everything's done already," I reminded Sammie patiently, determined not to answer her in kind and add to her stress. After all, I knew it wasn't directed at me. She'd gotten engaged to her college boyfriend a few weeks ago, and his family was coming to our family's home this evening for a meet-the-in-laws dinner. She was just nervous, wanting everything to go perfectly.

"What about vacuuming the downstairs?"

"Did it as soon as I got home from work."

Currently, I worked part-time for my father at the Westman Times, our local newspaper, which he owned and operated. I enjoyed helping out around the place, as well as learning the ins and outs of running a small town newspaper. I was also taking classes from our local community college, and between the two managed to keep myself busy.

"What about the bathrooms?"

"Cleaned and stocked," I assured her. "Harli Jean took care of them this morning before she left for school."

Harli Jean was our youngest sister. At fifteen, she was bright, pretty, a sophomore in high school, and well on her way academically to earning a scholarship to Colorado University, where she'd always said she'd attend. She and our dad were huge Buffs fans, and had been since she was a young kid and started watching college football with him.

I wasn't a big fan of football myself, and had no grandiose dreams such as attending CU or joining the Air Force, like our middle brother, George. He would finish high school soon, and was already making plans to enter the service upon graduating. Sometimes, I felt like the only one of my siblings without a firm direction in life. Sammie had graduated college two years ago, and had been employed as a teacher ever since. Teaching was her dream, and now that she and Jeff were engaged, it seemed her other dreams were coming true, as well. George and Harli Jean, although both younger than me, knew what they wanted out of life, so where did that leave me? With no steady boyfriend, undecided on a career, and still living at home while I figured out the next phase of life. It wasn't that I lacked ambition: I knew I wanted something out of life, and I thought I was headed in the right direction. I just wasn't exactly sure what it was that I wanted. My calling was waiting on me. When I found it, I'd throw myself into it wholeheartedly. I simply needed to figure it out first.

"So the dusting's done, the iced tea is made, dessert is in the oven, and the wine is being chilled...can you think of anything else?"

My tall, blonde sister straightened from where she'd been leaning over the table, centering plates and twitching linen napkins, making sure everything was just so.

"Nope, and you need to chill, sis," spoke up Harli Jean, who came sauntering into the dining room. "Here have a drink. It'll calm you down."

I laughed when she held out a can of soda pop towards our older sister. "I don't think that's going to do anything except get her more hyper, Harli."

"Ew, I don't see how you can drink that nasty stuff," Sammie said, wrinkling her nose in distaste. "Don't you know how unhealthy it is?"

"Sure tastes good, though." Harli tipped the can up to gulp down a big swig. "Mmmm mmm, delicious."

I laughed again, but Sammie didn't think it was funny. "Stop it, Harli Jean. Why don't you go find something constructive to do?"

"Hannah just told you everything's done, and it is," the teen responded. "Martha Stewart would approve. I'll go in the kitchen anyway, and see if Mom needs help.

"At least that'll get me away from you," she muttered as she sauntered off, stealing another sip from her soda can.

Watching her, I grinned and shook my head, but looked back over at my older sister in time to see worry cloud her vision.

"I don't know, do you think this looks okay? Jeff

said his mom can be pretty picky. What if it isn't good enough? What if I'm not good enough?"

"Okay, stop." Grabbing her by the hand, I drew her out from behind the table. "It's fine. Everything looks great. You're great, you and Jeff are happy together, and I'm sure that's all his parents really care about it. Now stop fussing and go upstairs and get dressed. You only have an hour to get all beautified," I teased, "and it may take you that long to get your hair and makeup perfect."

She looked like she wanted to protest, but I spun her around and gave her a push in the direction of the stairs to get her going.

"No arguments," I demanded. "Mom and Harli Jean have everything under control. Just go get ready. I'm going outside to talk to George and warn him to be nice when Jeff's parents show up."

Sammie stopped on the bottom stair, craning her neck to look back at me. "Thank you," she sighed in relief. "I was going to, but he'll listen to you better."

"I know, I have the magic touch with men," I smirked. "They're like putty in my hands. You don't have to worry about him causing any problems. Go on, get going, girl."

My older sister took to the stairs and I opened the front door, heading outside. George had finished cutting the front lawn, and was putting the mower away when I caught him.

"Hey, George," I called, waving my arm to get his attention.

He spotted me and extracted an ear bud from his left ear. "Yo, what's up?" he hollered back, bumping a hip against the big, stubborn door of Dad's workshop to force it closed.

"I just wanted to talk to you for a sec," I said, jogging over. "You know Jeff and his family are coming for dinner tonight, right? Well, Sammie's really nervous. She wants everything to go well, and—"

"I know, I know," my brother interrupted, rolling his eyes. "You want me to be nice to Jeff and use company manners in front of his family. I promise I'll be good. Jeff may not be my best friend, but I can play nice for Sammie's sake for an evening."

"Wow, how'd you get so mature all of the sudden?" I grinned, reaching out to tussle his short, curly hair.

"Stop that," my brother demanded, shying away. "I'm not a kid anymore, okay?"

"Sorry." I dropped my hands back to my sides. "What's your deal with Jeff, anyhow? He's a nice enough guy."

"I guess." Shrugging his shoulders, George shuffled his feet, keeping his gaze downward as if embarrassed about what he was going to confess. "It's just—she's my big sister, y'know? I'm not sure he's really good enough for her...even if she can be a major pain in the butt sometimes."

I couldn't disagree with that assessment. "She can be when she gets all frazzled, huh? Like now. Man, she's been driving me nuts all day. In fact, I was going to escape the madness and go for a little walk before Jeff's family arrives. That's why I said I'd come out here and talk to you. It was really an excuse to sneak off."

George's sandy eyebrows lifted. "You better get back in time to clean up before dinner. Sammie will not be happy if you show up dressed like that." His nod swept over my jeans, t-shirt, and Nikes. I didn't think I looked that bad, but he was right: Sammie probably would want me to change before company arrived.

"Don't worry about me," I said. "You just get in there and shower before Dad gets home. He'll be here any minute, and he's going to need to shower too."

"Yes, ma'am!" My brother executed a smart salute. "See you at dinner, then."

"Yeah, see you," I replied, and hurried off with a little wave.

I knew I was cutting it close—going for a walk with only an hour left till show time, and me still needing to change. However, what time I hadn't spent the past couple of days following Sammie's orders, I had spent cramming for an exam that was coming up the day after tomorrow. My brain was full, I was more than a little stressed by both the pressure and my sister's drama, and I needed a break.

I'll keep it short, and get back in plenty of time, I promised myself. Sammie will be so busy with her hair and makeup she won't even notice I'm gone. Nobody will...

Down the dusty country road I hurried. My Nikes kicked up puffs of soil that swirled around my feet. Running my hand idly over my neighbor's fence, I discovered its sun-warmed planks still retained the heat of the day. Behind the barrier, several long-limbed thoroughbreds ambled about, seeking the best grazing spots. Their curried coats gleamed in the early evening light, their shadows stretching long

Knight's Rebirth

over new grass. Despite the hectic pace of the past several hours, I felt my nerves quieting under the serenity of the country scene.

Until I saw *him*.

At first glance, I thought he was the leftover stump of a huge tree that had once towered over our neighbor's pasture. The tree was long gone, however; only its enormous stump remained to mark its passing. The story went that a couple of decades ago a lightning bolt falling from a clear, blue sky had struck the tree, felling it instantly.

"Strangest thing I ever saw," Mr. Cutter, our crotchety old neighbor, had once remarked to my father. "Wasn't a cloud in the sky. That thing just came outta nowhere. Tree didn't stand a chance. Nothing was left but that stump. Since it was too big to dig up, I cut up the tree for firewood and just left it. Been there ever since."

Now, all dark and knobby, the old stump crouched behind the same fence that guarded our neighbor's horses, set back about thirty feet from the road. While jogging past on a twilight evening, I'd sometimes catch a glimpse of it from the corner of my eye, and my overactive imagination would flash desperate signals that *something* was there: a bear, a wolf, a stray dog, a monk in flowing robes. For a split-second I'd panic—then common sense would kick in. Inevitably, I'd realize it was nothing more than that stupid stump fooling me again.

Since this had happened more than once, I actually didn't panic when I first glimpsed the stranger. Didn't, that is, until I took a second look and the apparition didn't vanish. His flowing, coffee-brown robes didn't dissolve into bark and knobs; his white hair and beard weren't fading sunlight glistening on old wood.

What on earth?

I was so shocked I stopped dead in my tracks.

Who is that? What is that?

Was I deranged to think I saw an old man leaning against a wizard's staff, the wind toying with his white hair and beard?

Staffs like that don't even exist! I told myself.

The wood was blue—not painted blue, but...blue. The top of the staff was carved into a life-sized hand, its palm up and its fingers curved around a small, gleaming object. I strained to make out what it was.

A moon?

Yes, the object resembled a miniature moon, one shining as brightly as its real counterpart, its luminescence shimmering in the vanishing light of day. Marring its glowing surface were replications of the dark smudges that mark the mountain ranges and dry riverbeds of earth's moon.

Who is this, and why does he have a staff with a teeny moon on top?

Was he an escapee from a traveling Renaissance Faire? Maybe he was on his way to one of those superhero/fantasy/comic book conventions and got lost, winding up here? Was he into some sort of odd role playing? Was he dangerous? Senile? Playing a joke? How could I tell? What should I do?

Run, came the immediate mental response. Maybe not my bravest course of action, but this person clearly was not normal and had no business being here, lost or escapee aside. I figured it was time to get the heck out of Dodge before he noticed me standing there. Then again, this would mean bypassing him, which he could hardly fail to notice. Did that mean I should go back the other way, try to find help? Or should I be brave, after all—play the Good Samaritan, call out to him, ask him what on earth he was doing in my neighbor's pasture? Or, as a last resort, should I just stroll on by as if I hadn't noticed him at all?

My mind whirled, but I think my decision was already made. If the stranger hadn't seen me yet, maybe he wouldn't until I was too far down the road for him to do anything about it. Unless he was actually an Olympic runner beneath those bulky robes (not likely), I doubted he'd be able to catch me. Those long robes, not to mention climbing the fence, would have to slow him down.

For better or for worse, my choice was made: I would try slipping past and sprinting for the house. Tensing, I gathered myself for the fast dash back home. Unfortunately, at the exact instant I was ready to bolt, a sly mountain wind rushed down the hillside, through treetops, and across grassy fields. It caught me, tugging at my clothing and sweeping out my hair in a long swirl of brown. Catching sight of that sweep of hair, the stranger's head whipped about. Suddenly, he was staring straight at me.

I felt a cold, sinking sensation, like the bottom had dropped out of my stomach. For a moment, I was mesmerized by unimaginable blue-green eyes: eyes that pierced my soul, eyes that summoned, eyes that beckoned. Beneath their gaze, part of me wilted, but the other part of me fought back.

Don't just stand there. Run, you idiot! screamed

the fighter inside, and I obeyed. Putting on a burst of speed I was off, racing for home and safety.

Made in the USA
Columbia, SC
26 January 2019